IS THIS HOW YOU EAT A WATERMELON?

IS THIS HOW YOU EAT A WATERMELON?

Zein El-Amine

RADIX MEDIA

NEW YORK

ISBN 978-1-7377184-2-0

Editor
Meher Manda

Interior Layout and Design
Lantz Arroyo

Jacket Design
Sarah Lopez

Printed and published in Brooklyn, New York by Radix Media.

Radix Media
522 Bergen Street
Brooklyn, New York 11217

radixmedia.org

This collection is the winner of the 2021 Megaphone Prize (formerly known as the Own Voices Prize), an annual contest dedicated to the discovery of urgent and interrogative works from debut writers of color.

For more information on the prize, see **radixmedia.org/megaphone-prize**.

—To Zaloom

CONTENTS

Sharife vs. the Party of God

<hr/>

I N COLD MONTHS SHARIFE SPENDS HER TIME ON THE OTHER side of the house, in the communal courtyard that opens up to the valley. In that expanse, she has her meals, makes her tea, and washes for prayers. Walking into that space you would think that it was decorated by Dali. A sink attached to the exterior wall with a mirror reflects the green valley back at it, giving the impression that the wall is opening to a lush landscape inside the house. A frayed towel hangs at an angle from a rebar jutting out of the wall. A bare lightbulb dangles from the concrete canopy like a misplaced idea. Sharife stores things that she wants to keep out of reach of her relatives in a straw basket anchored at an impractical height on the wall with a metal hook, which doesn't make sense since she is the shortest member of her family.

The other side of the house faces the heart of the village. There is a balcony that has been painted off-white with maroon trimmings. From that elevated vantage point, you can look out on a small rectangular plot, the main asphalt road that cuts through the town square, and the winding road that branches from it to the western reaches of the village. At the end of the tobacco harvest season, that small expanse between the house and the main road is covered with low-slung tobacco leaves, strung between wooden square pegs to dry. After the tobacco is dried, it is moved to a two-story building bordering it. There the tobacco is hung from the ceiling like giant brown leis. Come October, the field will be transformed again, the site of the annual harvest ritual. Large bulbous black metal cauldrons are propped on stones atop a fire to boil portions of the grain yield.

In the summers the balcony that looks out at that ever-changing terrain serves as Sharife's main perch, a place that she sweeps daily, where she drinks her tea and smokes her cigarettes. It isn't her first choice, she much preferred the courtyard with its view of the valley and the crusader fort. But she abandoned it for the balcony when the rivalry with her sister, who shared that space, reached an unbearable pitch.

Being who she is, a tiny tendon-wired woman with salt coursing through her veins, she reproaches and critiques whoever dares to get caught in her crosshairs. *Shouldn't you wear socks? Aren't you cold?* And under her breath, *These people let their kids run like wild animals. Or, aren't you so and so's daughter? Where is your mother? Let her come see you in this state. Aren't you ashamed?* As a woman who never married and never had children, she expresses whatever maternal instincts she might have had through caring for her nephews and for the children of other people. She does this in her own way, by chastising the parents for not caring for their kids and *setting them loose like livestock* as she informs anyone who stops by for her famous tea. Her tea is that good, enough to keep people returning despite being subjected to her venting sessions that leave no member of the village, or her own family, uncriticized of their conduct, their unsanitary living conditions, and how they abuse others, mainly her.

Sharife once lived in the room just below the balcony, one that still carries the characteristics of the original house: the cut stone walls, the exposed timber beams, and a decaying leaning closet. But because of her friction with her sister, she decided to ask her brother to have a room built for her separate from the house. The new room, which opens out to the courtyard, is small, six feet in width and twice the length. But it took more than three months to finish this tiny building because Sharife appointed herself as the general contractor and pecked at the workers all day long. Every week there would come a moment when one of the three laborers would walk off the worksite, march up to my uncle's room and beg him to get her off their backs for an hour or two so they could get some work done.

In July of 2006, Israel invaded South Lebanon in a military operation called "Summer Rain." The IDF always wanted to demonstrate their literary prowess to western powers by putting literary labels on their invasions—a previous operation was actually called "Grapes of Wrath." The poetics here lie in the fact that Lebanon does not have any rainfall in the summer. In fact, all the rain is confined to the winter months. So "Summer Rain" is code for planned carpet bombing. The plan was to subject the Lebanese to a deluge of destruction for seventy-two hours and rout out the popular resistance that had expelled them from the country at the turn of the millennium. They would destroy every bridge on the main coastal road that connected the rural south with the rest of Lebanon. They would strafe the countryside, flattening thousands of homes. They assumed that this would force the Lebanese to fight among themselves and blame the armed resistance. Then they would sweep away anyone who ever took up arms against them through a massive ground offensive. All in three days.

Things didn't go as planned and the war lasted thirty-three days instead of three. Everyone in the village left in the first day or two and managed to zigzag their way to the city or the mountains where they were taken in by relatives and friends. Some did not manage to make it as their convoys were bombed along the route.

Sharife's two brothers and their families packed up as soon as they heard the thunderous approach of the bombers. Sharife's nephews took turns running down to her room to plead with her to leave with them. Her answer to their pleas was the same: "I would rather die in my home than live in that city of strangers." Her brother made one last attempt after his family and their essentials were loaded into three cars. Sharife just dismissed him with a wave of the hand. "May God protect you, be on your way. I am too old to be spending what little of the time left on this earth scurrying around like a cockroach." They finally gave up and headed north to Beirut.

A chain smoker, Sharife rolled her own for three decades and then began to buy L&M cigarettes, an American brand, when homegrown tobacco was not as abundant and her arthritis made it difficult to roll. Her hyperactive daily routine includes several tea and cigarette breaks. She would sit on a low stool, gather up her scarf on her lap, extend her tiny head over the kettle and glasses and burn away the tobacco with the same intensity that she does everything else in her life. This is the only time that she is still. In between these times, she is a blur of activity. It is a mystery how much "housework" she could generate daily. The outside observer would think that she runs a whole household with children and such but it's just Sharife and her OCD. She would make a hundred-yard dash from morning until 2 pm, when she would knock herself out with a dosage of valium that could knock out a cow.

She depends on her nephews to buy her cartons of tobacco from the general store which is a short walk away. Every week someone coming in from the city would stop at the general store to get a carton for her. All in all, she has been smoking for seven decades, and the miracle of it is that we never hear her cough. Her brother jokes that she probably suppresses both cough and cancer through sheer hard-headedness.

Day six of "Summer Rain," drones buzzing night and day targeting anything that moved, and Sharife doggedly sticks to her routine. During nights, the villages are submerged in darkness as light itself is targeted especially if it is mobile. There are no innocent lights, all light is tried and executed on the spot. Everyone knows the drill: don't drive at night, not even a motorcycle, especially a motorcycle, don't turn on the porch lights, and shut all windows with wooden shutters.

Sharife sits alone in her tiny house, listening to the Arabic broadcast of Radio London on her transistor with the mangled antenna and manically eating her last piece of chicken, bone and all. She reclines on the wall, grabs her Bic lighter and her pack of smokes, tips her L&M hard box and out slips her last cigarette. She has never lost count of them before. Sharife curses the devil, puts the cigarette to her lips, winces as it sizzles and lights up her face. She looks under the bed and in the closet, looks around her small space, and peaks out at the courtyard. She curses herself when she realizes that there is no one else around to blame. She crushes the pack and asks out loud, "What am I going to do with myself?" She reaches under the bed and pulls out one of the many different-sized makeshift boxes. There she finds her silver flashlight with a slim long grip and a big bulb worthy of a headlight. She grabs the four size A batteries sitting on the window sill where she suns them to extend their life. She turns the flashlight to look into the bulb and switches it on but nothing happens. She examines the bulb and gives the flashlight a smack and it comes on. She is momentarily blinded. Even when she recovers her sight a few minutes later she can see the ghost of the filament seared into her retina. She curses the manufacturers of practically everything that she owns, the Chinese. "The Chinese are going to be the end of us!" She crosses the courtyard with the flashlight on and the last cigarette dangling from her mouth. She goes up to the second-floor balcony to look out over the main road. A drone buzzes above like a giant bee, but she is too fixated on the burning end of her last L&M to care.

Then she hears the sound of potential salvation, a whispering among men, and a stomping of feet on the move. The sound is coming from the south end of the main road but is buffered by the only house on that end of the village. She spots them soon after, about a dozen men, some in full regalia with helmets and all, and some in fatigues and t-shirts, one of them carrying a rocket launcher over his shoulder. The minute they reach the open road with the clearing on one side and the tobacco field on the other, Sharife sets her light on the lead man. In the first seconds of silence, she starts to wonder if the Israelis had reached this far, this soon. She moves her light along the whole length of the platoon. When she sees that they aren't accompanied by an armored vehicle or a tank, she is assured that they are her people. She moves her spotlight back to the lead man.

"Is that the Hamade boy?"

"What?"

"Is that the Hamade boy?"

"No, there is no Hamade here. For god's sake Haje shut that light off and go inside."

She moves the light to the source of the voice. "May God give you good health young men. Can one of you run down to Im Ali's store and grab me some cigarettes? I am completely out."

The man in the lead moves into her line of light and shouts through cupped hands, "Listen Haje, Im Kamil is hovering above us and we have to move on. For god's sake shut off that flashlight before that thing spots it."

"This thing?" ringing the flashlight like a bell, "This thing is nothing—this thing is practically a candle."

"We have to go Haje. Goodbye, go with peace. Shut off the flashlight and go inside, may God save you!"

"Do me a favor...aren't you a son of the village? Help out this old woman...I finished my cigarettes and I just need one pack. Just one, to tide me over until tomorrow. May God save you, my brother."

"Haje, we don't have any cigarettes and we don't have the time to get you anything right now. Hear that buzzing? That is an MK drone—they're armed these days. They shoot at anything that moves and any light that flickers. Do you understand?"

"Yes, but the general store is just two steps from here and Im Ali will open it up for you if you knock. I know that it looks like the store is closed but knock on the side door and she'll come down. I have an account with her so you don't have to pay, she'll put it on my tab. Just say that it is for Sharife."

"There is no strength but in God! Haje! We are in real danger— this lull won't hold much longer. We have to make it to the next village. For god's sake shut off that flashlight before they hit us. They can spot a candle from these drones...stop shaking the thing, may God preserve you Haje, stop shaking it!"

"The whole affair will take a minute."

The man turns back to the men as they try to stifle their laughter. "This is unreal, this same house was bombed in the last attack," he tells them and waves to march on.

"Are you the Party of God?" Sharife shouts at them.

"What?" the man answers knowing what she just said but cupping his ear for the insult.

"You call yourself the Party of God?"

"What is your problem woman?"

"The Party of God, you say? More like the Party of Satan! Go ahead, march." She rings the flashlight like a marshaller guiding a plane into its dock, "March on to red hades if I care! If it wasn't for this catastrophe that you got us into I wouldn't be without cigarettes."

"Unbelievable, let's go men!" the leader of the platoon waves them on.

"Go! Why should you care about a miserable old woman like me? Why should you care if I die of deprivation? Am I a fly to be swatted? I am just going to go into my dark room and wither away. Is that what you want? You want me to wither away in darkness…" her voice trails off as she slowly realizes that she is talking to the now vacant street.

Someone shouts from the neighbor's house across the way, "Go in Haje Sharife, I hear them buzzing again. Go in, God preserve you." A mistake, as Sharife turns her searchlight to the houses around her, trying to locate the source of the voice.

"Turn the light off!" the voice shouts.

"God curse you all," she whispers and turns the flashlight off, "There is no humanity left in this world."

She goes back through the house to descend down the back stairs to her room. She resumes her search, turns the place upside down trying to find a single cigarette to no avail. She walks out into the back courtyard and sifts through the ashtray and finds a cigarette butt that still has a stub of tobacco on it and carries it back into her room. She sets it on her window sill and considers when she should smoke it. As she does this, she hears the sound of a boy yelling below the balcony. She hurries to the metal gate next to her room and peers through a square opening at its center, which is at eye level to her five-foot stature.

"Who's that?" she calls out.

"It's me Haje, I brought you cigarettes."

She winces at the boy in the dark but does not recognize him.

"How did you know I needed cigarettes?"

"One of the men that just marched through told me. I was knocking on Im Ali's place and he gave me money and told me to run a carton to the old lady at the end of the road. I think he meant you."

She scans the boy head to toe through the peephole. He looks left and right, shuffling his feet as if he has to pee. This makes Sharife suspicious and she hesitates for a minute then opens the gate. Sure enough, he has the cigarettes, not just a pack but a whole carton, and not any carton but her brand of choice, L&M.

"May God preserve your hands," she tells the boy. "God bless you and bless the resistance. Let me give you some money for it."

"It was paid for. I need to run back home. My mother is having a fit," he yells as he runs back home. Sharife peels back the cellophane, tears the end of the carton, pulls out the pack, gives it a couple of taps on the back of her hand, pulls out a cigarette, lights it up, winces with relief, and exhales, "Gratitude be to God."

When "Summer Rain" ended the landscape was littered with hundreds of bombed-out homes and villages, every single bridge along the coastal road to Beirut was destroyed, farmland was scattered with cluster bombs. All the families returned south to settle back in the villages. The first weekend after the end of the war, there is bumper-to-bumper traffic on the few intact roads heading back from the cities and northern mountains to the rural south. Some already knew that their homes were hit and yet they return with mattresses strapped atop their cars because they still want to spend their weekend in the country like they did before, even if it meant sleeping on the floors of the skeletal remains of their ancestral homes.

Sharife's relatives were safe with the knowledge that she had survived the assault because they had contacted the Red Cross and were assured that although the balcony of the house was hit in the last days of the war, Sharife was alive and kicking.

The man sent by the Red Cross knew the village well. He was dispatched with another man to check on her. The two men entered the courtyard from the valley side and found a dented and burned water tank in the middle of it and called out for Sharife. She had been praying in her room which seemed intact except for the curtains which were shredded by fire, singed strips waving in the breeze. Sharife emerged cocooned in her prayer white wrap, bundling her tightly wound scarf on her head sealing all her graying hair from view. Without a greeting, she launched into a long lecture about knocking and announcing oneself before entering. The startled volunteers realized that they would have to let her finish and return to report that she was ok. Only after the lecture did she pause to ask, "What is it? What do you want?"

"Only to ensure your health and safety."

"Ok, you ensured, now go with peace. You could have ensured my health weeks ago when I nearly died for lack of cigarettes and food, there would have been some use for you then. No, but you wait until those dogs bomb the Karake house next door, launching the water tank into the courtyard and blowing away my windows setting my curtains on fire. It is a good thing I took my valium that day because I slept through the whole thing. Look at this mess," she complained, pointing at the tank and scattered chunks of concrete, "no amount of sweeping can clean this stuff. I've swept for a week and nothing has changed."

Sharife's brothers make their way back along with their families, three cars in a row, in a line that backed up for miles. They stop at a coffee shop, just before the final turn to the village. They heard that the general store in Deir Keifa was out of almost everything.

Sharife's nephew Wissam enters the coffee shop and finds it empty except for the owner behind the counter and a handful of men in civilian clothes gathered around a table sheltered by a grape arbor. The customers are sipping tea and talking loudly as if they had been served spirits. They had that air about them. Locals could always tell who belonged to the resistance even after they shed their military garb to return to their farms and their mechanic shops and businesses.

Wissam greets Abu Hassan the owner, "Al-Salam Alaykum"

"Wa Alaykum Al-Salam," Abu Hassan replies.

"A carton of L&Ms if you please."

"Here you go. You're from Deir Keifa, right?"

"Yes."

"Oun's son?"

"No, his nephew."

"I know your uncle. You look just like him when he was your age."

Suddenly the men's chatter comes to a halt and all turn to examine Wissam. The oldest one among them, a man with a broad tanned face, receding hairline, and a closely trimmed salt and pepper beard, motions to him with a flick of the wrist. "Come here, I want to ask you a question."

Wissam walks up and greets the men.

"You're from Deir Keifa?" the man asks.

"Yes."

"Is your house the second one on the right past the Husseinieye?"

"Yes."

"Do you have a grandmother, yay high, that stayed there during the fighting?"

"Yes, that's my aunt."

A young man sitting in the back of the circle leans back his chair, a cup of tea steaming in his hand, and asks, "So where were you during the war?"

"We all went to Beirut."

"And you left your aunt behind?"

"We asked her to come with us but she refused. We begged and pleaded but she has a hard head."

"Really?" The young man interrupts him scanning the men as they break into laughter.

"Yes...you have no idea."

"No, we do."

He looked at them puzzled, waiting for the other shoe to drop. The older man waves at him to come closer so that he can speak directly into his ear. "Listen to me son, the next time this happens, do your country and the resistance a favor and take your aunt with you."

Is This How You Eat a Watermelon?

THE KIDNEY WAS SECURED AND THE DOCTORS WERE READY TO operate on Ghassan the following morning. Not one, not two, but three doctors stand at the foot of his bed. Ghassan is tired and nauseous but the sight of them amuses him. When they begin to talk, he narrows his eyes and melds the triplets into one body. The fact that their speech was rehearsed and sequenced for maximum effect, as if coordinated by one body and communicated by three heads, helps enhance the illusion. The doctors are channeling his older brother Kamal, the Minister of Labor. He can see Kamal sitting in their office, knee over knee, his bodyguard stoic beside him, giving the three-headed hydra stern instructions on how to approach Ghassan. "You have to handle him like an adolescent, he is in his forties but he is a child," he might have said. Each doctor has dealt with Ghassan at one point or another in the past few years because of his various health crises: kidney failure, liver problems, diabetes, and high blood pressure. So they knew how to deal with him, but they would have been obliged to sit and listen and pretend to take notes out of fear of the minister.

Ghassan loves his food, his drink, and his family, or shall we say, families. His first wife was a Lebanese woman, Souad, a childhood friend who was always amused by Ghassan's carpe diem attitude that infuriated his family. She saw this as innocence, not immaturity, nor recklessness, and adored him for it. She gave him three kids, two boys, and a girl. Ghassan was in his element when he was with his children. It allowed him to roll on the carpet, play in the mud, be a ravenous eater, and liberate his inner Tasmanian devil. This caused problems sometimes, especially during weekends spent in the south, in their home village of Assawane. Having the wilderness nearby, with its climbable fig-trees, abandoned forts, hidden wells, renegade beehives, scorpions, and snakes, raised the risk of Ghassan's antics. However, he did not need to leave the house and put himself at risk, he can do wild all by himself.

Take for example the watermelon incident. One day Ghassan was sitting playing checkers with his youngest daughter Huda, who was seven at the time. They were in the courtyard of Ghassan's ancestral village home and were using the backside of the backgammon box to play. Souad brought out a tray of watermelon slices. It was a June afternoon of bearable dry heat, so they sat in the cool shade of an old lemon tree that arced over them, laden with lemons. Ghassan looked up and saw Huda nibbling along the top of this red semi-circle of a slice that dwarfed her face.

"Is this how you eat watermelon?" he asked. She looked at him puzzled and waited for clarification.

"Is this how you eat watermelon?" he repeated. She started to worry, as he was not using his usual terms of endearment.

Then he added, "Do you eat it like this?" and imitated her nibbling. Huda looked back at her mother for help and caught her stifling a laugh.

"Do you eat a big slice of watermelon like a bird, like this, nm nm nm?" he pecked at his slice with his nose, pinkies raised.

Huda broke out in a smile that prompted Ghassan to explain. "You eat it like this, like a goat," and Ghassan went into typewriter mode, chomping wildly at the slice from one end to another, watermelon seeds flying left and right. So daddy's girl took the tip and ran with it, imitating him, putting her whole face into her slice of watermelon, filling her mouth and nostrils with it, digging in deeper until the rind curved up around her face. She looked up at her father with a long red smile that extended up to her ears, watermelon seeds entangled in her curls. He rewarded her with a pat on the back and kiss on the top of her head.

Two days later the family was back in Beirut. They arrived late at night and Souad put the kids to bed. She returned to check in on them and noticed that Huda was snoring. She joked about it with Ghassan, "She is even taking on your snore, God help us." A week later Huda was feverish and was having difficulties breathing at night. They called the family doctor and he diagnosed her with asthma and prescribed some holistic treatments including weekends in the mountains.

But two weeks later Huda was still laboring with her breath, day and night, so they took her back to the doctor. This time, the doctor located the problem with a cursory examination.

"There is a seed lodged up her left nostril," he told Ghassan with a smile and a shake of his head, "The damn thing is sprouting!" The doctor anticipated Ghassan's accustomed hearty laugh, but Ghassan just stood there with a look of terror on his face. "I can take it out right now without putting her under," the doctor added.

Ghassan crouched in front of Huda, pinched her cheek, and said, "It won't hurt habibti." The procedure took less than half an hour. The doctor put the extracted seed in a jar and told Ghassan that he should keep it to preserve this memory for her. Years later, when Huda will leave home to attend Lebanese American University, she will take the jar with her.

One night, as Ghassan was plowing his way through a mezze table at the Barometre, the owner introduced a Palestinian debke troupe and announced that they will be a regular Friday gig. One of the dancers caught his eye—a woman dressed in a traditional black dress with red and green tatreez embroidery. He noticed how serious and focused she was as she waited to get in the circle and how she came alive as soon as she entered the fray and led the troupe. Ghassan's cousin Ali noticed his attentiveness and introduced them after the performance. The woman, Rana, did not take to him right away, mainly because Ghassan was uncharacteristically uptight in her presence, and partially because Rana was not putting up with any posturing from strangers that night. Nevertheless, Ghassan was smitten and he woke up thinking about her the next morning. He started to keep track of her through Ali, turning every topic of conversation between them into an inquiry about her. Beirut being Beirut allowed him to have many "chance encounters" with Rana: at movie festivals (although Ghassan did not have the patience to sit through foreign films), book fairs (although Ghassan was not a reader), and benefits for the refugee camps. Eventually, after several of these "accidental" encounters, she started to notice him and warm up to him. His humor began to flow easily and she responded with her mode of flirtation—merciless sarcasm that whittled away at his charm.

Several months later, after one of her performances, Rana sidled up to Ghassan at the bar after changing.

"What can I get you?" he asked.

"Tonight is not an Almaza beer night nor is it a Johnny Walker night, tonight is an Arak kind of night."

"Oh really?" Ghassan replied.

"Yes, definitely an Arak kind of night," Rana asserted, slapping the bar with every word for emphasis.

"And why is that?"

"I don't know, maybe because the world doesn't matter to me tonight."

They drank Arak and snacked on mixed nuts. He kept his ego in check, she tempered her acidic critiques, and they were connecting for the first time. At a pause in the conversation, she looked up at him in silence, closed her eyes for a second and looked down at her drink, and up at him again. She asked him for a cigarette. They stepped out into the courtyard, which was under renovation at the time, and into the blaring horns of Beirut. She went through the cigarette so fast that Ghassan had a hard time keeping up with her. She dropped the butt to the ground and stepped on it with the force of a dabke stomp. He followed suit, assuming she wanted to go back inside, but when he looked up from putting out his cigarette her face was inches away from his. She cradled his head with both hands and kissed him. What stayed with him from that night is not so much the kiss itself but the way she held his head. She stepped away as violently as she had surged at him, a strand of sweat-swept hair across her brow, her V-neck linen shirt askew, olive skin twinkling in the streetlights. She told him that she was in the mood for "the village," for the rural South. It was past midnight on a weeknight so he assumed that she was hinting at a weekend trip and offered to take her on one during the coming weekend. She fixed him with a serious look and said, "No, I mean now, I am in the mood for the village now." It took him a minute to understand what she was proposing but when he did he put down his drink, took away hers, and headed for the door. She was behind him, pretending that she was not following, stepping on people's feet while apologizing left and right.

They drove on the coastal road with the Mediterranean to their right, the flash of the moon panning the ocean, riveted by their reverie. They went through Sidon then skirted Tyre in a record hour and headed southeast from there. The car hugged the hills, the valley close enough to make one dizzy, no guardrails, no markers, and no lights. The sea breeze—cooled by the limestone cradles in the foothills—moved through the car. They drove through the villages of Jouaiya and Deir Kifa until there was nothing but the narrow ribbon of road laid across rolling hills. As they rounded an arid stone-pocked hill, a moonlit cornfield opened up in yellow glory. Even before the car came to a full stop, Rana bolted out and ran into the field. Ghassan ran after her. She kept disappearing and reappearing in his path, black hair moving among the blonde silk-tufted cobs. Then the clothes started coming off. Ghassan lost sight of her but followed a trail of garments: a tossed white linen shirt rendered fluorescent in the moonlight, a bra snagged on a stalk. A shed shoe almost nailed him in the head, and a pair of deflated jeans served as the last marker on her trail. Ghassan started stripping too, tripping over himself with every item, shedding clothes that he had bought that same week: pointed-toe cowboy boots from Red Shoe, a Pierre Cardin linen shirt, and charcoal Guess jeans from the GS store. He found himself naked and disoriented for a moment, the stealth rustle of her flight gone. Then he heard her singing a lullaby: "*Tick tick tick, yam Slaiman…tick tick tick zawjik wane can?*"

He moved towards the source of the song and then stopped as the singing stopped, then it started again: "*tick tick tick can bil-Ha'li'am yuqtuf jawz wrimaan…*"

He almost tripped over her laying in the fold of the field, parted corn stalks like an open book on both sides of her. Her skin shimmered with sweat, hips wider than he imagined, breasts gently jiggling as she labored with her breath through laughter. They were voracious in their lovemaking and they were at home with it, nothing orderly about it, nothing graceful, comfortable in its clumsiness, but well punctuated with the synchronicity of its completion. He laughed as she wailed a combination of nonsensical curses that involved God, the Prophet, and Ghassan's mother; no one left untainted, desecration all around. They lay, in their fuck-flattened clearing and looked up at the sky in silence. Ghassan crawled on all fours looking for his pants, disappeared into the thicket, located the cigarettes, crawled back into the clearing, and jutted his head between her bent knees, two lit cigarettes in his mouth. She laughed and he sat cross-legged like a pudgy little Buddha, the cigarettes sticking out at angles from his puffing lips, waiting for her to stop so he could give her one.

Within months of that encounter in the fields Ghassan left his wife. Although he could afford an apartment in a prime neighborhood anywhere in Beirut, Rana refused to leave the camp where she lived most of her life. Much to everyone's shock Ghassan moved in with her. So instead of living on the very cosmopolitan Al Hamra street, within reach of his favorite cafe du jour (t-marbouta), his favorite beach club (The Officer's Swim Club), and the restaurants he loves, he made a home of a second-floor built-up apartment. The place was of questionable structural integrity, precariously balanced atop a general store, entangled on all sides with a spaghetti mesh of illegally installed electric and cable TV wires, a back porch with a view of an open sewer. A small place but a sunny one lit up with Moroccan pastels that Rana had painted with the help of a friend.

Many people thought that this move would force a change in Ghassan's lifestyle, that Rana would be the one that would tame him and get him to settle. But it took less than a year for him to get back to his old habits. He went back to his daily dips in the pubs and bars, and a diet that consisted of charbroiled meats, raw kibbeh, and dairy-heavy sweets soaked in rose water syrups. He was soon diagnosed with diabetes and started having fainting spells that landed him in the hospital. In the year that followed his diagnosis, Ghassan was rushed to the hospital three different times for various reasons: asthma issues tied to his smoking, liver problems tied to his drinking, and dizziness brought on by exasperated diabetes. Repent, repent, the doctors begged and he just smiled and nodded in his hospital bed. Days after his release he went back to his habits. Relatives would spot him on the streets at night, shake their heads, and mutter to each other, "God help his family."

Now he sits here facing the multi-headed medics. One doctor—a tanned man, full head of gray, the type that spends his afternoons at the St. George's Hotel pool-side, playing backgammon—conjures up a look of concern and demands, "We need to know that you are on board." In return, Ghassan gives a sorrowful nod, pretending to play along.

"Very well, here is what is going to happen after tomorrow's operation—for at least the next six months you have to refrain from alcohol and smoking. You will be placed on a strict diet for the next year. The list of prohibited foods and suggested meals is here, and I will give it to your family. Lastly, and this is the most challenging bit, you will have to wear a mask over your mouth and nose for the next three months."

All three doctors wait for a reaction, but Ghassan does not flinch; his pleasant demeanor does not turn murky as expected.

"Are you still with us?" the doctor asks.

"We have to do what we have to do, God help us," Ghassan answers with a shrug. The doctors leave and, on cue, Kamal calls to say how happy he is that Ghassan has been so cooperative, but turns stern at the end of the conversation with a warning. "The time for playing is over, Habibi. This is serious. Think about Ziad, think about Abdullah, think about Huda, and you will get through it."

The call from his brother came at six in the evening. At midnight Ghassan goes to the bathroom, gets dressed, walks down the hallway without looking around. By now he is familiar with all the off-the-beaten-path corridors, stairwells, and exits. Additionally, as a resident smoker, he knows that there is a back exit to the hospital that would put him out on the side of the Corniche and that there is a guard there that he must get past. He knows the guard by name, so he salutes him and asks him for a cigarette. They smoke and chat for a bit and then Ghassan hands the guard a roll of twenties in dollars because he knows that he has been paid extra to watch him and call if he were to leave the hospital.

"What is this for?" the guard asks.

Ghassan winces as he sucks down his cigarette and answers, "For your memory loss," in an exhale of smoke that wafts over the guard's face. The guard hesitates, but Ghassan signals at the rolls of dollars to help him decide. The guard nods at Ghassan and opens the back gate.

Apparently fear of the minister trumped the sum of the bribe because the guard ends up calling Kamal anyway. The minister's personal bodyguard, Mimo, is dispatched to locate Ghassan and get him back to the hospital. Mimo was a childhood friend of Ghassan who had actually given the bodyguard that nickname when they were teenagers. Mimo's real name is Muhammad, a man with such a massive body that he carries his own climate. He has the brawn of a bouncer and the brains of a sleuth. It takes him three days to locate Ghassan. A tip from a bartender at the B-018 bar comes at five in the morning and Mimo puts in a call to Kamal and then to Rana. It is Rana who gets to the location first but cannot figure out where the bar is. She scans the buildings for signs of commercial stores but they are all residential. As she crosses a clearing between the buildings, she spots Ghassan emerging from the B-018. When one says, "emerging from the B-018" it literally means rising out of it, as the hip bar is a converted underground bomb shelter with a concrete roof that is flush with the ground. Its roof is equipped with hydraulic pistons that tilt up the massive slab to allow for a view of the sky and the stars. It was not unusual to see people staggering out of the B-018 in the early hours of the morning but this was way past closing time. Ghassan walks in her direction but does not recognize her until he is a few feet from her. There is no exchange of words, just a look of exasperation branded on her face. He puts his arm around her for support. They walk towards the car quietly, she holds him around the waist and he leans heavily on her. She opens the door for him but he stands there looking at her. For a moment, he is focused, and asks, "Where are we going?"

"Home," she says.

"Home, home?" he asks.

"Yes, home home," she answers.

"Not home hospital?" he asks.

"No, home home," she repeats in resignation.

Rana starts up the car and Ghassan slumps against the passenger door. "I am in the mood for the village," he mumbles.

"Really," Rana answers, stopping the car.

"Yes really, let's go now. I don't want to go into the city."

Rana turns around and heads to the coastal highway. Ghassan rolls down the window and manages to heave himself high enough to prop his chin on the door and let the wind run through his curly hair. Just past the airport, south of the city, they pass a mountainous pile of concrete rubble. "What is that?" Ghassan asks, nodding towards the pile that blocks his view of the sea.

"You don't know?" asks Rana.

Ghassan narrows his eyes as if trying to recall something.

"How many times have you passed this in the last five years?" Rana asks.

Ghassan doesn't answer and tracks the dumpsite as they clear it.

"It's the rubble from the 2006 war. They hauled it out here when they were rebuilding and haven't done anything with it yet," explains Rana, "you've passed it every weekend since then and you never noticed it?"

"Pull over," Ghassan says, yanking on the door handle.

"What is it?" Rana asks.

"Pull over, I am not feeling well," Ghassan yells as he opens the door and waits for the car to stop.

He runs down to the sandy beach and stoops over, hands propped on knees. Rana looks at him through the open door then turns her sight to the Mediterranean as he starts to retch.

The Sayed and the Snow Woman

SAYED ABDULLAH WAKES UP UNDER A MUCH-LOVED QUILT JUST like the quilts that cover his nephews and the futons that span the entire floor. So "loved" that it has faded to a shine revealing the second layer underneath that contains the stuffing. As there is little that can't be sensed from the confines of this room, his read on the weather outside is that the morning chill of the past few days has been broken, not by the sun but by something else. He can hear it, something he has not heard in a decade and certainly not around here but in the Faraya mountains. Yes, there is the rooster with its own ever-shifting standard time. Yes, there are the hypnotic coos of the doves that would lull you back to sleep. Yes, there is Abu Musa in the distance firing up his tractor. But there is something underneath all these familiar sounds, a perpetual chafing that the kid in him, always there beneath the prop of public respectability, can instinctively recognize. He bolts out of the bed, leaps over the footboard, grabs his abaya and his scarf, and runs out in his leather closed-toed slippers. By the time his wife Taj can mumble "What is happening?" Sayed Abdullah is already beyond earshot.

Above them, on the second floor, Abdullah's older brother Oun puts on his slacks, white shirt, thick wool socks, leather slippers, and a wool abaya that he drapes like a cape not bothering to slip his arms through its sleeves. He walks down the concrete steps that turn at a right angle all the way down to the lower courtyard where his brother is now standing, face upturned to receive this miracle that continues to come down like a hail of cotton. Midway down the first set of steps, there are three bare concrete masonry blocks cemented to the wall like lego, leading up and away from the staircase to a worn dark gray wooden double door that seemed to have been placed by mistake in the center of the great cut stone wall. It looks decorative as opposed to something functional. Three steps and Oun reaches the doorknob and enters the room. Inside he looks at his nephews sprawled out on the futons, that will later be rolled up and put away during the day. Past them is his sister, her futon placed by the window on his right. His mother's bed is empty as she woke up with the dawn prayers and went about her work in the kitchen and grain cellar. And lastly, he can spot his youngest sister at the far end of the room, on a raised bed. He closes the door behind him to prepare for the big reveal. The two boys are perfectly positioned for the surprise as they are both asleep facing the door. He watches as the younger one, possessed with a constant electric current, moves in his sleep in slight epileptic jerks. The older one cocooned in the quilt is buried up to his forehead in the fold.

"Good Morning!" he exclaims and pushes the door open. The boys struggle to their elbows, rub their eyes and wince at the sky. At first, they cannot distinguish the snow from the cloud cover. They rub their eyes to check whether this is just an apparition from the static of sleep. Then they realize that these specs, traversing open space, are snowfall.

"Snow?" says the younger boy and they both stand up and scan the scene, their uncle holding them by the shoulders, the boys oblivious to the chill nipping at their bare feet. The whole valley to their left has been dusted, the rooftops on the outskirts of the village all white, the pine trees, bordering the compost heap that is referred to as the Hakoura, are ringed with the accumulating flakes. They rush back inside and put on the homemade sweaters that their aunt made them and corduroy pants that their absent mother bought them. They slip on their thin socks and bruised bulbous shoes and make a run for the door. They step down the lego block stairs with their uncle in the doorway bracing them by the armpits so they don't fall in their excitement. Before they run down to the courtyard, their grandmother yells to them from the balcony to return: *come and get a bite to eat before you run off!* They turn around and step up steadily, swaying with each step in disappointment. In the kitchen upstairs they sit on the floor with the big brass platter before them, filled with Labneh, halloumi cheese, tomatoes, zaatar swimming in oil, and leavened fresh Arabic bread. Their aunt stands in the corner, stacked tea kettle steaming on the two gas burner cooktop readying the tea. She scalds the Turkish tea glasses with masterful turns of her fire-proof fingers, spoons the sugar then pours tea liquor from the top porcelain pot, and tops the glasses with the hot water in the lower aluminum kettle. They take the bread and roll an "aroos" (a bride), a slim burrito of labneh and zaatar, and run out to the balcony to watch the snow. The aunt complains that they will get indigestion if they were to eat and run around but they are mesmerized by the sight of the white powder that has now covered the whole scene beyond the balcony wall, the slope down from the house, the valley, and the slopes up to the crusader castle on one side, all the way up the village annex on the other side.

They stop short of the stairs and decide to set their cups of tea on the balcony wall to watch the scene. Sayed Abdullah is busy below them gathering the snow in the lower courtyard. The top of his head is totally exposed except for the fine hair that was now plastered to his temples from the melting snow. The curled flat licks framing his temples bring to mind Roman emperors with their coiled crowns.

At first, he struggles with the shape of his creation which keeps sloughing but then, as the temperature drops, the snow starts to adhere and things start to take shape. The two boys love watching him in his child mode. But what really rivets them, far beyond the desire to frolic in their first snow, is that they realize that he is not making an inanimate object but a human likeness, something that is long forbidden by Islam as any attempt to imitate god's creation is considered blasphemous. This is why Arabic calligraphy is so intricate and varied, as Muslim artists put all their creative energy into that craft to refrain from painting the human figure. But they don't know that the forbidden aspects of Sayed's work are about to go beyond that. At first, they thought that the broad base of the snowman was merely a structural feature but then they begin to make out a curve of a waist sloping up to a generous bosom. At that realization, they stop mid-chew and look at each other, wide-eyed with amusement. This is ice-cold sin taking shape before them. At that point they hear a voice from below, a familiar mournful one: *the wind is going to slap you like that, come cover your head, may God preserve you.* The boys realize that Taj has been watching the whole scene. There she is berating her husband for not covering his head, while she herself is bare-headed, naked hair hanging for all to see. Taj would never go out in the open with her head uncovered. There would always be at least a white muslin scarf wrapped loosely around her head. But she now stands in the doorway to the kitchen bracing the doorframe on one side as if expecting an earthquake, fixated on the sight of her husband creating another woman. She has that look on her face, a mournful one that teeters between weeping and laughter, eyes with a twinkle of a smile, mouth straightened with sorrow. Everyone that knew her knew that look.

Abdullah doesn't even look back. With one hand he keeps shaping the sloughing snow on the curve of the hips and with another he fishes in the pocket of his thobe for his cap and places it askew on his head which lends more mischief to his appearance. World gone wonky, the Sayed is touching temptation, and his wife is uncovered to the world. The world askew like Sayed's cap. To the kids, it feels as if the snow has unfurled the inhibitions of the couple.

Abdullah now gathers a fistful of snow and gently pushes it onto one of the breasts while holding onto the back. From where his wife stands it must seem like he is having an intimate moment with the frozen bust. Taj suddenly charges forward in socks and flip-flops. The kids have never seen her move that fast before. She gets halfway to her husband before her feet are set sideways in a slide that brings her a few feet closer before she completely loses her foothold. Her flip-flops go flying behind her as she slides, hands first, towards the Sayed's feet. She skids on her stomach, like a seal emerging out of water, before coming to a stop at her husband's ankles. Abdullah jumps around and attempts to pick her up before she does a split and falls back, taking him down with her.

"Have you lost your mind?" Abdullah says as he stands up, feet straddling her supine muddied body, and tries to lift her up again, this time managing to heave her by the hands, grab her around the waist, and twirl into the momentum of the lift. These two were always affectionate in their own subtle way but never displayed the slightest bit of public affection and here they were entangled in a tight embrace as they struggled for balance. They both start laughing as they steady themselves and walk back to the kitchen with Abdullah bracing Taj by the waist and Taj holding on to his shoulders. The couple disappears below the children's perch and the boys turn to each other in silent bemusement. These kinds of things are not talked about. They wait for the couple to emerge from the kitchen or for Abdullah to engage in some sort of game as he usually does but that doesn't happen. They look out on the valley and see that the snowflakes are now getting fatter. They take this shift to mean that the snowfall is going to intensify rather than diminish because they don't know that this is because of a rise in temperature, not a drop. They watch as the snow woman's face goes askew as if turning her head in question. She leans sideways into her diminishing waist and juts out her hip into a final flirtatious pose before collapsing.

Groom

B

ASSAM'S WEDNESDAY NIGHT RITUAL WAS INSTINCTIVE, SOME-thing leftover from years of partying in high school. A futile ritual driven by unsubstantiated optimism. A mechanical one, where a college kid living with a workaholic father, drives home from college with a pavlovian promise of a good time, merely because of the day of the week. That day would be a Friday in the west but here it is a Wednesday, marking the start of the weekend. Hopped up on anticipation he races in his Chevy Malibu, V8 engine growling at the straight desert road, devouring the asphalt in a 20-minute straight ride between two worlds. One world, an exposed concrete fortress of a campus on a hill on the edge of Dhahran, with sandblasted buildings that Korean workers took years to unpolish, doing the work that the frequent sandstorms would have done anyway. The other world, with green manicured lawns straight out of the Florida suburbs. One, of men and more men, a sea of white thobes, black veils, and lingering glares; the other, a world of color and sprinklers, swimming pools, and movie theaters. One where nothing was allowed, the other where everything was permitted, in secret. Both worlds devolving into dysfunction in their isolation.

This futile ritual would go like this: Bassam would get home after spending the week in his room on campus. He would take off his sweat-soaked t-shirt and dust-rimmed jeans, take a long bath, and get dressed. He would go through motions that were no longer necessary, grooming, perfuming, and dressing up in silk and linen shirts, hip-hugging slacks, brass buckle belts, Italian leather shoes.

The futility of this ritual does not set in until he ties his shoes and sits back on his bed. Here he would remember that he has no-where to go, that he just got dressed for an occasion that does not exist, that there are no occasions for this dress or this state of mind and he would start to despair at the empty evening ahead of him.

But for the past two months, things have been different. In some limited way, this routine was given purpose. It was two months ago to the day that he stopped on his way home from the University to pick up his brother from the American Consulate School. He had finished his day early and thought that it would be fun to give his brother a ride home. He loved surprising his brother. As he waited near the minibusses that ferry off students to their fortified compounds, he spotted a woman in the passenger seat of a bus parked perpendicular to his car. She was talking to the driver which was unusual, as the drivers were generally invisible to all, especially to the expats. Then she turned around and gave instructions to the students, or at least it seemed that way. Bassam assumed that she was either a visiting college kid or a young parent on chaperone duty. He maneuvered his Chevy to get a better view of her. There was plenty of room to park between the bus and the retaining wall. He pulled up and waited to see if she would turn around. She finally did, after one of the students pointed him out to her, probably with some snide remark. Bassam waved to her. She smiled and then turned her attention to the student again. There was a lightness about her, a freckled face framed by strawberry blonde hair that at that moment was lit by the merciless mid-afternoon sun. She turned to Bassam and waved back, as if she knew him. Then, to his surprise, she slid open the bus window and gave him a cheerful "Hi!" He rolled down the window and asked if she was the chaperone for the day. She laughed at him, rolled her eyes and told him that she was a visiting college student substituting for her mother.

"Picking up this child," she said jokingly, pointing to a girl that he couldn't see because her head was in a book. He told her that he goes to college here and that he lived "on the base," which expats knew meant the American base. Then he pointed to his brother now walking down the sloped sidewalk to the parking lot and mimicked her. "Picking up this child."

The bus began to move forward and stopped when a stray student was heard shouting, "Wait! Wait!" Bassam moved backward keeping his hands on his lap, eyes on the girl and she responded with a giggle. "Bassam," he said, pointing to himself then pointing at her.

"Cindy," she responded as the bus moved beyond his sight. He kept reversing, following her movement. She settled in the rear of the bus, and as he passed her, she slid her window open and shouted, "See you later!"

They saw each other again, a few days later, at the same spot. It was then that they had a long conversation and arranged to meet at her house, where she lived with an absentee father like his. Soon they began meeting two or three times a week and since dating was punishable by prison, they usually hung out at her house or drove around town without disembarking for fear of the religious police who would ask them to produce proof of marriage on the spot or be hauled away until the parents or sponsors could be located and reprimanded. In her case, her father could be detained indefinitely for his daughter's indiscretion, that is until the American Embassy could interfere.

Now Bassam drives to her house, Cindy Lauper squeaking through his makeshift silver Sansui car speakers that he had installed in the back. She is usually home on Wednesday nights but her father and stepmother are out for the early evening and that is when they usually meet. He arrives to find her gate unlocked. On pushing the door open, Bassam finds Cindy sitting on the stoop set in a concrete courtyard. A tuft of spiked hair bobs behind her but she sits unfettered, head bowed over her knees. She tilts up her face and smiles at him without a word. But it is not her regular southern California sunshine smile, it is a more mature smile that evokes resignation and sadness. He walks around her to see what is going on and she lifts her hand from her lap in a motion that he reads as "tread lightly" so he stops. Crouching behind her sits a monkey, huddled against her back, busy sifting through her scalp. It is a scrawny one with a long sad face and wispy gray fur that gives the impression of having suffered an electric shock. The monkey sifts gently through Cindy's long strawberry blonde locks, picking at her exposed scalp and nibbling her imaginary lice with exaggerated puffs of his cheeks. Bassam watches, as if in a trance when suddenly, the monkey locks eyes with him. It seizes its sifting and turns its back to him. Bassam registers a familiar fear in the animal's eyes, a déjà vu moment that he can't place. The monkey leans its shoulder into Cindy's back but keeps watch of the man, it marks him with a side glance and then turns away in a disgruntled huff as if willing him to disappear.

Something about the way the monkey's behavior feels like a blow to his body, it deflates Bassam. The monkey turns to Cindy and she responds to what seems like telepathic communication, her expression switching easily from alarm to sympathy. She turns to Bassam with a stern look.

"Stay where you are," she commands him and goes back to attending to the monkey, stroking the soft hair on its back and whispering in its ear. The monkey relaxes enough to turn its back to her as she begins to groom him. Cindy pats the ground behind her motioning Bassam to sit down. As he settles on the steps, he remembers the instructions that he received as a lifeguard on how to approach a drowning person. How you should always move in a wide circle, keep your distance, until you get behind the person and then reach over their shoulder and under the armpit, move your hip up to their lower back and swim sidelong to the nearest ledge or shore. The reason for the caution is that a drowning person will likely try to grab you and climb on top of you to keep from drowning. It is a basic survival instinct. At this point, Bassam felt as if he was maneuvering around a drowning person and he did not know why. In their silent ritual, these creatures were somehow speaking directly to his body, constricting his throat and knotting up his upper back.

"He came over that wall an hour ago," she finally explains without turning to him. Her voice emitting from a place deeper than her throat, strained like she is pulling back on something, or pushing down a cry.

"I don't think he likes men. He is afraid of them, so don't come close." The monkey keeps Bassam in check as Cindy grooms him. He doesn't want to stay put, he is drawn to the pair and their ritual. He wants to be part of the huddle, he wants to groom and be groomed by them. He feels that the monkey will make an exception for him, and will take him in. He moves closer, with a lifeguard's caution, until he is sitting on a step higher than the two and stares meditatively on the ground sifting through an onslaught of sensations. Something creeps up within him and then falls back. Something that has been pressed down and piled on for years, something that has been operating on him stealthily. Whatever it is, it is crowning in his throat now and a mixture of fear and loss is clouding his sight. The monkey keeps looking back to mark him but Bassam knows now not to make eye contact, lowering his sight to the ground in a submissive motion.

The monkey twists his torso to look at Bassam again and makes a huffing sound that could be read as hostile. Bassam maintains his bow and doesn't budge. The monkey then moves slowly towards Bassam who has his head lowered in submission. Bassam's breathing becomes labored, he was not one to trust animals at all, he fears stray dogs and stray cats and has had a couple of encounters that confirmed his fear. The monkey slowly moves one hand against the stiff straight hair on the back of Bassam's head and picks at his exposed scalp with the other hand. Bassam slowly slides to a lower step to allow the monkey better access. He relaxes his shoulders and his breath settles into a yogic rhythm, he feels the warm belly of the monkey against his back and is comforted.

"He has been abused by his owner," she said.

"Who?"

"Sam," she answers.

"Who's Sam?"

"That's Sam," she points at the monkey with a playful poke.

"Who's his owner?"

"The man who lives two houses down."

"How do you know where he came from?"

"I've heard him scream at times when I walk by that house."

"Scream?"

"Yeah it was a call for help, it wasn't like a monkey playing with its owner. It was like it was being beaten or worse?"

"Worse?"

"Yes, worse," looking at Bassam with raised brows as if he should know what is worse.

A grating sound of metal announces itself from one of the doors down the lane. The monkey turns to the girl and hides its face in the back of her armpit. She quickly embraces its small body and shushes it tenderly. Its whimpers are muffled by her body as it shakes in fright. Then there is a shuffling of feet in the sand, the slapping of flip flops as a man speeds up his gait. The sound stops outside the iron gate. Then, silence. Cindy gathers up the monkey and retreats into the house. Bassam peers under the gate to spot a pair of dusty sandal-clad feet pointed in his direction. The feet linger for what seems like a long while, then they turn to the side and the gate gives in a little from slight pressure. Bassam thinks that the man must be leaning against the door to listen in. This goes on for a few minutes, with Bassam frozen in place before the man shuffles on. Bassam monitors the movement of the man as he stops at the next gate at the adjoining house and repeats his eavesdropping before he returns to his home and shuts his gate with a loud clang. Bassam waits a little longer to make sure that is the end then goes into the house. He finds Cindy sitting in the small foyer and tells her that the neighbor is gone.

"It's OK now, it's OK," she whispers to Sam while looking up at Bassam. Sam climbs on her lap to hug her and nuzzle the crook of her neck. Cindy is now looking at Bassam with sympathetic eyes and he is confused as to whether she is comforting Sam or him. She reaches up to hold Bassam's hand and he pulls on it, thinking that she needs help getting up but instead she gives his hand a squeeze and says, "I think that you should go home, I'll call you later. OK?"

Under any other circumstance, her rejection would have wounded him, but he isn't surprised by her request this time; he is struck by the maturity of the declaration. Where was the cheerful girl from Pasadena? The bubbly one. This is a woman on her guard, operating on maternal instincts. Bassam nods and considers kissing her goodbye, but arrives at the quick conclusion that it would be inappropriate at the moment. He walks out of the gate, scans the desert terrain, looks up and down the street to make sure that the coast is clear before getting in his car. He drives to the base but doesn't feel like going home so he continues past the main gate and heads toward the beach. The empty road compels Bassam to drive faster, his V-8 engine gobbling up the asphalt ribbon stretched out across the desert road. As he speeds past the sand dunes, a memory percolates to the surface by the hypnotic undulation of the sand, a thought buried for years: a darkened room, a dining room table, and a cold calloused hand moving below it, touching his yet hairless thigh.

Killdeer

'VE COME TO BELIEVE LIFE HAPPENS IN LOOPS. HERE I AM HEAD-
ing down Route 2 just south of the sound and fury of the city,
only this time as a poet-in-residence, taking the same road that
I took a decade ago as a quality control engineer for a runway proj-
ect at the Patuxent Naval Station—my introduction to Southern
Maryland. I used to work four days a week, twelve hours a day, and
leave on Thursday evenings to a one-bedroom apartment in DC.
On the one hand, St. Mary's County felt familiar with its tobacco
fields, and the smell of cured leaves reminding me of Lebanon, but
on the other hand, here were people that, to this day, grew a row
of cotton shrubs along their white fences as a nostalgic symbol of
the *good ol 'days.*

An engineer then, a poet now. In between, a great transforma-
tion from a person who tried to fit humanity into rigid formulas to
one that had shed those cold calculations to become immersed in
the nuances of the human condition. I make a note on a pad that
I keep on the car's dashboard: "Life in Loops," remembering the
times during my commute when I would pull over to put down
thoughts that percolated on the long drives back and forth.

I can tell it is the drying season by the way the barns are loaded with tobacco leaves at different stages of decay, some still green popping against the maroon barns, some already browning. Some barns had their doors wide open and some had their backs turned to the road, slats missing, strung tobacco peeking through.

I'd hesitated when I received an opportunity to spend a week as a writer-in-residence at the southernmost tip of Chesapeake Bay, at St Mary's College. I had just come by a substantial freelance job with the American Bar Association. But now, half an hour into my drive, I find myself shedding all reservations. I shut the radio off after the signal veered to an evangelist ranting about the end of days. I cracked the window and the October air voided my mind's chatter about overdue tasks left behind and that vacuum began to fill with words and ideas. The Chesapeake is lit up with the low afternoon sun. I felt the warmth of its reflection on my face, the nourishment of the sunlight, a tingling waking me up, *a wedding in my blood*, as a favorite poet would have put it. I looked to the left and saw the pathways to the campus, each cutting through the wetlands that form most of the campus's landscape. Wind-combed long grasses, bushes, and shrubbery busy with birdsong. I never could identify flora or fauna and I made a mental note to take advantage of my stay here to read up on my birds and trees.

The cottage reserved for the artist-in-residence is just off a country road lined with poplars in their wispy detonations. I pull into the dirt road and park in a clearing between the house and a converted garage. The keys are there under a rock below the deck where Ari, the head of the English department, left them for me. I pause at the deck for a minute and survey the surroundings, mainly the long grasses that hug the house on two sides. The field is bordered by spearhead-shaped pines that make me think of the pines that shaded my childhood home in South Lebanon. Once inside, I'm unimpressed by the gaudy furniture but taken in by its size. I tour the place recalling all the tips that Abi, a friend and previous resident of the house, listed in an email to help me make the most of this experience: the house is ancient and tends to groan at night, the best part of the house is the modern extension, the hikes in the nearby colonial park are glorious. I believe it was Abi's recommendation that gained me a quick acceptance to the residency. We have been friends for many years, and our friendship unwound over drinks at the only neighborhood bar on the historic U Street that was yet to be discovered by the gentrifiers that have flooded DC and erased every last trace of that street's historic Black renaissance. Every time we entered this place, the bartender—a young Somali man, would offer the setup for a joke. "An Arab and a Jew walk into a bar…" he'd say and trail off. At times somebody who had started drinking at Greenwich Mean Time would attempt a punchline that would inevitably be insulting to us both.

I drop my stuff at the cottage and leave for a bite and end up backtracking to Stoney's on Broome Island for their famous crab cakes. On my return, I find Ari waiting for me on the deck, sitting on a fold-out chair, feet up on a stool. I remember that I was supposed to meet with him half an hour ago and that we had even talked about going out to dinner. I walk up to him shaking my head and smiling and he catches on that I had forgotten about the appointment.

"Don't worry, it happens all the time, people get here and get lost in the place," he says before I can offer any apologies.

"Sorry I was hungry and anxious to hit one of my favorite spots," I say, taking his hand and opening a fold-out chair. "Can I get you something?"

"There should be a couple of beers in the fridge left over from the last resident," he says. "I won't mind one if you don't?"

"Perfect, I got it."

We sit drinking and talking about the schedule for the upcoming week. I light a cigarette and stand away from him at the corner of the deck.

"Abi tells me you work as a translator," he says.

"Yes, translator and interpreter," I answer.

"What kind of translation?"

"Whatever falls into my lap: documentaries, court documents, literary works. I've even worked with Pulitzer Prize-winning journalists on stories for *The New Yorker*. Last year I got stuck in Beirut while visiting family and ended up working for almost all the major western media outlets."

"Really? You mean you were stuck there with Bourdain?" Ari jokes.

"Yep, never met him. I wish. But unlike him, I didn't heed the American Embassy's call to be shipped out of the country when it all began. I was dreading how the US media was going to report on this. So I just stayed until the bombing reached Beirut then I went down south, into the fire, so to speak. I ended up holed up with reporters that had turned a seaside resort into their headquarters."

"Did they ever leave the resort?"

"They had to. It was hit and they scattered all over. This was the first time reporting was close to the truth. Mainly because they'd go report on a bombing and then the bridges would be destroyed—cutting off ambulances that were rushing all over to keep up with the casualties. The reporters would be stuck there with the wounded. I saw an ABC reporter locate a kid under the rubble and pull him out with our help. I doubt he could've put his usual spin after that."

"Yes I did notice a difference in reporting on that war, even on CNN."

"I think the most sobering thing for these reporters were the hospital visits after the invasion. There were horrifying stories coming out because of the cluster bomblets that IDF had scattered all over the fields as they retreated. Those things attracted kids with their colorful ribbons in blues, yellows, greens. They were all over the wheat fields and tobacco fields and even hung from grape arbors and apple trees. The hospitals were full of children who had been maimed by them. One kid lost both his legs and told reporters an unbelievable story about being dragged from the fields into a roadside ravine by a dog that left him in a puddle of water visible to traffic. He claimed the dog intentionally put him there to snuff out the fire that had engulfed his legs. He gave a description of the dog and told us to find him and give him some meat as a reward. His parents told us the same story except they didn't believe this dog existed but they weren't about to deprive their kid of his coping narrative."

"Were they able to remove the cluster bombs."

"That's nearly impossible. There were over a million of these bomblets scattered all over the agricultural areas. The UN sent a special team to try to detonate as many as they could. By the way, those bombs were made right here in Maryland."

"I did read something about activists protesting at the headquarters of the company that made them. They put red dye in the water fountain in the courtyard. The visuals were amazing."

"Up in Rockville, right?"

"Yes, I believe so."

"I left South Lebanon with a New York Times reporter and along the way we saw the clearing operation and how it was going to be impossible to accomplish. We watched UN soldiers crawl through a corn field with knee pads and protective vests. They were taking the cluster bombs to designated detonation spots. I am not sure how they managed to get anything done because those things had mercury sensors that set off the bombs at the slightest tilt."

"Do you write about that experience?"

"No, never been able to."

"You should."

"People tell me that all the time, especially when I tell these stories at social gatherings. But I get to my desk and rarely manage more than a paragraph or two. I feel I'm nibbling at the edge of something, unable to plumb the depths. I haven't given up though. I'm sure I'll break through at some point, it just takes time."

Ari gives me a rundown of my responsibilities which are minimal: I have to lead a lecture for one of his classes, facilitate a creative writing workshop, and do a public reading at the end of the first week of the two week long residency. He acquaints me with the peculiarities of the house and gives me a list of his favorite hangouts in the area including bars, restaurants, and parks. He leaves with the promise to have dinner after the "compulsory reading."

The next morning: after an hour and a half of tractionless writing, I decide to drive to the trail Abi told me about, near the colonial museum, a mile along the shoreline. Supposedly the perfect spot for her daily meditations. As I enter the woods I'm immediately enveloped by maple trees at their peak red. I stop, close my eyes, and listen remembering why I love October—the perfect temperatures that need not be tinkered with, the deep sleep on cold nights, the ever-changing sky with dabs from a divine palette.

But this was the quietest trail I'd experienced: the sounds of the woods, its birds and burrowing creators, the rustle of leaves—I hear nothing. There's no sight or sound of life. I feel as though the trees are ensnaring me. My breath turns labored as if the leaves are sucking the oxygen instead of releasing it. I once described the wind twirling red leaves as tongues ululating in welcome but now they feel like red flags that outflank me.

After a half-hour hike, I spot the water through the trees and I am anxious to open up my view to its expanse, to escape the claustrophobia of the woods. But when I emerge on the shore, I see that the body of water is only a small muddy bay covered with a soggy algae carpet, its surface gelled and stagnant. The wind shifts inland and I wince as a stench coming off the water reaches me. It isn't the smell of fish nor of sea vegetable. Whatever the source, it makes me think of decomposing flesh—great masses of it. This is where Abi meditated daily? I scan the silver surface of the waters but can't see any bloated bulges or birds eating carrion. The glint off the still waters could have been pleasant on any other day, on any other shore, but here it is blinding, not the kind that you receive with closed-eyed bliss but a threat, like the flash of the white lights of a cop car or the night flares that were frequently dropped above refugee camps back home. I continue to walk along the shore but the stench follows. Even when the scenery gets more pleasant, the odor does not let up. Nausea creeps up on me and I decide to turn back. I remember a prophetic dream that I had when I was twelve, where I was accompanied by my brothers and we were crossing the border into Lebanon and stepped into a charred landscape under a sky perforated with multiple moons. I say "prophetic" because I had that dream a month before the Lebanese civil war set that country on fire. I note down the memory in my Field Notes pocketbook.

> *Where there is supposed to be mountains turbaned*
> *by stagnant clouds, there is instead a plain*
> *darkened, not by the earth's spin but by extinguished light.*

My train of thought is interrupted by an alarming staccato screech. I cup my ears to it as it does not sound natural. I feel it in my teeth as one would receive the clawing of fingernails on a blackboard. I turn to my left to find an open field of feathered ferns lit by shafts of light but can't locate the sound. I scan the emerald expanse and locate a sole wing fluttering among the leaves. I immediately recognize the bird from the days when I worked construction in Northern Virginia. The Killdeer. It protects its nests set on the ground from advancing humans by distracting them with its sudden flight to a nearby clearing where it smothers itself into the dirt and flails about on a wing as if it's injured. When the bird has earned the human's attention—and sympathy—it flies away, having successfully maneuvered the distraction. An expert actor of the skies. The sight of the wing shaking amidst those leaves sends shivers down my spine. I turn to move away from it, but the bird would not cease its screeching. I glue my ears shut and run farther and farther away from the godforsaken shore, the tight embrace of red trees, the dank smell, but the scream of the killdeer pierces right into my mind. Late at night, alone on my bed, I can still hear the Killdeer, ringing in my ears.

I am a tired boy the next morning but rally to make coffee. I eat a bagel with cream cheese and drink the coffee at the kitchen counter trying to swim up to the source of the disturbance that should have dissipated in the light of day. There are no remnants of the dream world that can be gathered to build on this morning. I refill my cup and carry my coffee to the "writing room" as Ari called it, an addition to the old house that extended into the pine-bordered grasslands behind the house. The spacious room has blonde laminate flooring, a handmade rocking chair made of twigs and branches and one long drawerless desk that sat against the window. I settle with pencil and paper to shed the distractions of the laptop. I stare out of the window, at the field beyond and wait for inspiration. An image of a woman running in a panic comes to me, and with it, a first line—

> *Like the moments before the bombs*
> *unzip the sky with a whistle, followed*

by the tossing of the earth and a mother
running…"

Before I can jot down the first few words, those that are usually pregnant with possibilities, I sense a movement in the periphery. I turn to spot the wing of a killdeer shaking in an epileptic fit near the edge of the field. I scan the whole horizon to find the source of its threat but there are neither mice nor men. I push up the window and catch its unsettling screech. It seems to rise in volume changing the whole scene from a sunny field into a landscape of Lynchian dread. I close the window, muffling the cry, and return to the page. It's meaningless—I've lost the hook to bury into the poem. I end up reading several drafts of poems I'd discarded which only remind me why I put them in my "Dead Poems" folder. I pick up my laptop with the intention of sifting through some drafts that can perhaps jump-start me but instead I go down a rabbit hole of tangential research, answering emails, and surfing Instagram. The morning is shot so I head to the university on foot, hoping something will come as it always does on long walks that create a vacuum that sucks inspiration out of thin air. I spend the afternoon crisscrossing campus on walkways set above wetlands thriving with life: unseen frogs, egrets, and tadpoles. There is poetry there, set on stands at different lookouts. Although it's all maritime poetry I can't relate to, I still appreciate the holistic aspect that it lends the place.

October evening comes with that steep temperature drop that kills the chlorophyll and creates those brilliant reds. It also plays havoc with old houses like this artist's residence. For several nights, I am awakened by the creaking of the floorboards, moaning of the columns, and shifting of the beams. Whatever was nagging at me at the start of my residency is magnified as sleep deprivation whittles away at my emotional and creative capacity.

Midway through my residency, I am scheduled to read to the university's English department. Having produced nothing of note here, I decide to read the poems that were mentioned on the flyers for the event that were posted around campus. I start with one I wrote in the year that I lived in New Zealand titled "Aotearoa" which is the name that The Maori use for the country. "Aotearoa" for the land of the long white clouds. I hadn't planned on starting with this poem or even reading it at all, but since Ari used it in the promotional poster, I made a quick decision to kickstart the evening with it. This was about a poet's inability to pen down the beauty of the place. Lines—about the *pirouetting Pohutukawa trees*, the *gurgling streams*, and how the *hissing stars kept the poets awake* but stumped—were met with looks of confusion and disruptive whispering among the audience.

Next, I read a whimsical number that is a crowd pleaser at readings, a poem about teaching windsurfing in Barbados at a time when I didn't know the first thing about the sport. But not a peep comes from this crew—no laughter at moments that usually draws it and no signs of delight at the recitation of the beach songs that were sprinkled throughout it. It's almost as if there is a gap between the poetry they are expecting and the poetry I chose to read to them.

Then it hits me. This audience wants to draw blood. They want war. They expect violence from a Lebanese poet and the Q&A confirmed that desire.

"Have you written anything about the recent wars in Lebanon? What do you think about the turn of events," asks a student from the first row.

Another History major introduces himself as a "self-confessed Middle East nerd," and wants to talk about the Lebanese Civil War. "How can Lebanese literature and *your* writing in particular shed some light on the Lebanese Civil War? Over 100,000 people died," he says, a hint of know-it-all pride in his voice.

"I would answer that if my poetry had anything to do with the Lebanese Civil War," I say. I explain that the poems I shared today are simply about my love for the natural beauty of New Zealand or my adventures in scamming British tourists.

"Besides," I continue, "it is not poetry's responsibility to shed light on events the world chooses to ignore." But that does not seem to satisfy them and they keep up the siege.

Finally Ari intervenes and tries to provoke the students to think outside the blood.

"Why should writers who lived through war and occupation be confined to it?" he asks. "Maybe they want to write about poppies or unrequited love or their cat."

Ari makes sure to find me after the reading with apologies on his tongue.

"I assure you, my kids are much more open-minded than they demonstrated tonight," he tells me.

It is my turn to forgive him. "I merely experienced today what every non-white writer experiences at least once in their career," I say with a tight smile. We go to dinner afterward as originally planned and commiserate about bombed readings and even sadder Q&As.

"So, how's the residency treating you?" Ari asks.

"I am unable to sleep well although October is really a month of exquisite slumber for me," I admit. "It is also a time where I turn into a whirling dervish of creativity but I have been in a state of paralysis since I arrived." I tell him about the killdeer, how they had seemingly overtaken my experience, interrupting my poems, turning long walks ominous.

"Killdeer?" he asks.

"You know the bird. Does the whole broken wing performance when you accidentally approach its nests."

"Yes, that bird."

"They seem to be really touchy here, more than I had encountered," I say.

"Touchy?"

"Yeah, nervous. They panic even when you are not posing a threat to them or the nest. They keep going off left and right and at the most inopportune moments."

"Where?"

"One was on the hike near the colonial museum and several times they pop up in the back of the house when I'm not anywhere near them. It's frustrating because they go into their frenzied act whenever I sit to write."

"Hmm, I have never heard anyone complain about that before.

But I could see how it could be a bother. I have to consult my Birds of the Chesapeake book about this. It could be a seasonal phenomenon."

⟪∵⟫

The days drift on with nothing coherent to show for as I jump from genre to genre. I follow false starts on poems before abandoning them to write the opening graph of a short story but the energy that propelled that opening quickly dissipates into informational language, so I leave it all to take on the mammothian task of outlining a novel but that proves to be far too ambitious an undertaking. I return to the poem once more and this time I envision—or remember, it's hard to know for certain—a sandy field bulging out of the earth as if a giant is about to emerge from below.

> *A slow heave*
> *where*
> *the seconds*
> *stretch and snap*
> *and everything*
> *is left to gravity.*

But the poem fizzles out with each line, its image turning blurry, defying clarity, and I start to wonder if it's me who is unable to muster the image. An old therapist's advice comes to me, to recognize this sort of avoidance by checking in with my body. Through a process called EMDR, the therapist taught me to correlate the location of tension in the body with the incident that is being recalled to parse it out from present experience. I am aware of the knots in my upper back and tightness around the back of my head that stretched into the nerves around the ears and all the way up to the temples. I know that it has to do with something that happened back in 93 but I can't recollect if I witnessed it or was told about it.

⟪∵⟫

In the last days of my residency, I take to giving out scientific assignation to things that were creeping me out, in order to render them impotent. I remind my rational self that the evening groans were the expansion and contraction of the aged hardwood floor planks. Drafts exist in all old houses. They come from the attics that funnel the air or from invisible cracks in the window frames that are too old to be completely sealed. The sporadic gasps I have been hearing must be from the ancient floor heating system on its last breath. The strange calls at night—that staccato screech followed by three short bursts—are a paranoid killdeer trying to alarm and disorient predators as a survival mechanism. This nightly rundown helps me get through another day, but I am still sleeping less than I needed to, unable to produce any coherent work. I jump from line to line but have no idea if they are connected to visions or experience. My writing always comes to an unintended dark dead end. I know darkness lends dimension, but the quality of this one snuffed out any splendor to the story and stilled the heartbeat of any character, it flattened rather than enlivened.

One night in the residency, I sit on the deck, sipping on my ritual glass of scotch when I reach into my pocket to find a joint. I remember that Abi had given it to me before I left. "One for the road," she had said and tucked it into my front pocket. I smoke half of it then snuff it out on the deck rail and go up to bed. Halfway into a page of a novel, despite all the noises of the old house, sleep finally comes.

I dream I'm moving through grasslands that could be either South Lebanon or Southern Maryland. Silence abounds. Here and there, yellow ribbons flutter above the grass and then fall, flutter and fall, to the tune of the killdeers and their screeching. At first, a handful here and there pop up in alarm then the whole field boils with them—a cacophony of sound as hundreds of ribbons rise and fall in discord. I wake up to find that I had slept for a full nine hours, the first night in two weeks. I decide to leave right then and there and get my coffee on the road. It was the last day of the residency and I had intended to wait until dark to leave but I had begun to feel agitated, anticipating the daily disruptions that have been murking up my meditations.

I pack what little I had brought with me, return the keys to their place under the rock and walk up to the car. I stop in my tracks when I hear that now familiar call again and for a second I think it's a remnant of my dream. I turn to see a killdeer doing its thing, the whole injured act. It irks me to no end as I am nowhere near the grassland that must house its nest.

"Ok, let's see what you're hiding there," I call out to the bird, annoyed. The further I get from it the more frenzied it gets. Two blind steps into the tufts of grass and I hear a crunch. I raise my foot to find four crushed eggshells bleeding yellow yolk. With a mechanical move the killdeer straightens itself, freezing all its flaying in one second. It side glances at me in silence, then opens its beak to emit an uninterrupted shriek. I put my hands to my ear and the bird's cry turns to a human wail within the enclosure. There in the full light of day a woman runs through my memory reaching out for something beyond my vision. I turn to the killdeer and it is no longer flapping. The bird stands there looking at me but the sounds echo in my head as I recognize the woman and what she is reaching for.

I make my way to the car and throw my bags in the trunk. I peel out onto the road with a cloud of dust that settles on the poplars. When I get to the highway I start to decompress, something that usually happens when I am traveling in the opposite direction, away from the city. The further I get the more relaxed I become until my mind is swimming with unmoored memories. An hour into the drive I get to a point where the highway splits into two and forms a triangular area around a clearing where the Amish set up their farmer's market once a week. I had been writing words here and there on the dashboard paper pad but now I had a fully conceived piece that was crowning. I pull over and turn my full attention to the poem and all the moving parts start to gel.

> *Like the moments before the bombs*
> *unzip the sky with a whistle, followed*
> *by the tossing of the earth and a mother*
> *running to snag her boy busy dribbling*
> *downfield. Throwing up the whole*
> *lot like a sandbox. A slow heave where*

> *the seconds are stretched and snapped*
> *and everything is left to gravity. Earth,*
> *with its ready embrace, not knowing who*
> *to catch first, the boy or the mother,*
> *or the water-cushioned child about*
> *to be unborn into this tossed-up world.*

A dam was breached and intact images sail through, ones that I cannot look at directly because it would be like staring into the sun. They can only be spotted in the peripheral vision like certain stars. I pull over twice more to note the flood of fragmented memories—the last of these stops was at a precarious spot on the shoulder of the beltway. By the time I get home the whole story had been spawned. It is a journey taken by four boys traversing a familiar landscape that has been scorched. It is a prophetic dream that predicted a long bloody war denoted by surreal scenes of skies with multiple moons that are like *cataracts in the eye of an absent god*. It is of a pregnant woman running in a futile attempt to catch her child that had been flung like a rag by a fury of falling bombs.

Send My Regards to Your Mother

I SOMETIMES REFER TO MY COLLEGE YEARS IN SAUDI ARABIA AS "doing time." But early in those years I did "do some time" that almost did me in—and my mother, too.

I had spent high school in Bahrain as a boarder. My father then pressured me to attend university near our house in Dhahran, where he worked as a contractor on the US military base.

I kept in touch with a few high school friends that first semester. Every Wednesday evening (our Saturday night), I would come home, shower, shave, put on dress clothes and walk over to the international call center. There I would make two calls, one to Diana and one to Karen. These conversations felt like conjugal visits although they were not of a sexual or romantic nature. They were the highlight of my week in a country where dating is illegal and alcohol is prohibited, at a men-only university with nothing to do on weekends but dial-up these friends a mere 15-minute flight away. It was the 1980s before the causeway was built between the two countries, allowing people to drive across the Gulf and indulge in all things forbidden in Saudi Arabia.

One weekend I decided to hop on a plane. The next morning at Diana's house, I had a great breakfast of omelets, labne, olives, and tea, not knowing at the time how precious the meal would be. I dressed in jeans and a T-shirt reading, "That's right, we baaaad!" I grabbed my baby blue OP tennis shorts and headed off to meet another friend for a match.

Zigzagging to my destination, I came across a housing compound much like the gated communities that dot the island. This one looked new, with a red-and-white striped guard shack at the entrance. The shack was unmanned though and the gates were wide open. I could see clear across the property to the tennis courts. I decided to take a shortcut.

As I exited the back gate, a military-uniformed guard came running through the compound to catch up with me. When I turned around, he shouted, "Waggif!"—and then, unsure of my native tongue, "Stop!" He caught his breath, pausing at the sight of the bundled OP shorts. He asked me a question in what I gathered to be Arabic and switched to broken English. I remembered that Bahrain contracted Pakistanis to serve in its military, and made a mental note to joke with Diana about how Bahrain gives guns to people who speak neither the language of the natives nor that of most of the expatriates. I gathered that I was trespassing somewhere I should not have. The guard was sweating up a storm in his dark wool uniform and cap. Trying to end his misery, I put on my best authoritative voice. "I am a student...American embassy....Play tennis...Manama American school." I waved my blue OP shorts like a bullfighter's cloth. Then suddenly he said, "OK. Go."

A few minutes later, a military jeep skidded in front of me, blocking my path to the school. As the dust settled, I moved my arm away from my face to see a Bahraini soldier in a gray uniform glaring at me. "Inside!" he repeated. I spotted the Pakistani guard and two other soldiers in the jeep and knew that whatever explanation I had given him was not sufficient. I had a feeling that it would be futile to challenge the soldier at this point and I decided to get in and see where this took me. I was confident that I could find someone who would listen and allow me to dispel any kind of misunderstanding I had with the Pakistani soldier. One of the soldiers in the back slid out of the car and pointed to the backseat.

I got in and the soldier got back in and shut the door. I was sand-wiched tightly between two soldiers, their woolen dress chafing my arms and the scent of sweat and excrement filling my nostrils. The driver sped away like an ambulance on call.

When he finally slowed down, I glimpsed a high, whitewashed, fortified wall. The jeep moved through a metal gate with a concrete archway and passed a tower-like structure sitting on a concrete slab. It looked like a decapitated lighthouse, with no windows and no sign of a door.

I was escorted into a building so drab it looked abandoned. We walked up to an office with a male secretary wearing a thobe and headdress, a cheerful fellow with tanned skin and a bright white smile, one too fixed to be trusted. I got the impression he was expecting me.

"What is your full name?" he asked.

"Zein Mohammad El-Amine," I answered, adding my father's name.

"Stand there," he said, pointing me toward uniformed minders.

An Indian "tea boy" went into the office behind the smiling man. The door to the office was left ajar and I could see someone sitting behind a glossy dark mahogany desk dressed in a traditional headdress and white thobe. The thobe was draped with a dark brown wool abaya with gold thread trim. From his graying goatee and gaunt, shriveled cheeks, I guessed the man was in his sixties. The desk seemed a bit too large for him. He signaled the guards to bring me in, each one holding an elbow as if I needed assistance. The official continued to sign papers. I noticed a name plaque— Al Khalifa, meaning he was a member of the ruling family. I was anxious to speak with someone who spoke a language I could un-derstand. I was anxious to return to Diana and go out about town, have a laugh about the whole thing over a pint of Double Diamond beer and a double scotch.

"What is your name?" he finally asked.

"Zein El-Amine."

"What is your full name?"

"Zein Mohammad El-Amine," I said

"What is your father's full name?"

"Mohammad Bakir El-Amine."

He looked up at me for the first time since I walked into the office. "What were you doing at that house?"

"I was taking a shortcut to the tennis courts," I said.

I was about to explain further when I noticed that his attention had turned to the graphic on my T-shirt. He narrowed his eyes and moved his lips slowly, "Daaat isss... rrrright. Weee baaaad!" On the shirt was a cartoon of two intoxicated cats laying about trash cans in an alleyway, one with a bottle marked with a double X, the other with a limp cigarette or a joint drooping from his upheld paw. The word "bad" was indeed spelled with a half dozen vowels. The man did not seem pleased with this declaration. He looked up at my face, still squinting with distrust. I hastened to say that I was visiting from Saudi Arabia and started to reach for the military base ID in my front pocket. As I stepped forward, Mr. Khalifa pushed himself away from the desk and the two guards jerked me back by the elbows. "Stay where you are," the guard on my left snapped. The official turned the card over in his hand, in a way that told me that he either did not understand its significance or did not care. He set the card down on the desk and mumbled something to the guards I did not catch. The guards led me out again by the elbows and the smiling receptionist traded places with us, closing the door behind him. We stood in silence for long minutes and then the man emerged, still with the smile. I thought they had come to their senses. But what the grinning man said next sent my heart into freefall.

"Empty your pockets."

I hesitated. Having watched way too many American law and order type shows, my first response was to request a phone call. I actually said, "I am entitled to a phone call."

Smiley beamed at me. "Oh yes, you will get your call. You can call whoever you like."

My joints were turning to jello from elbows to knees. I did not have much on me—a few Bahraini dinars for lunch, my trusted military base ID, which I felt was my only ticket out of here, and compacted remains of a Kleenex. He checked the pockets of the shorts and pushed them back toward me. "You can keep this," he said and handed back the shorts.

The guards were at my elbows again, leading me to another part of the building. We went down to a basement with unpainted, roughly finished concrete walls and dim fluorescent lighting, and then into a room smudged with soot. There was a man sitting with a cigarette and a pile of papers and an ink blotter. Without inquiry, he asked me to come around. I stood shoulder to shoulder with him and he grabbed my hand to fingerprint me. He asked me to hold up a placard with a number and some scratches in Arabic. I did not read the scribble until they took the picture. "Suspected terrorist," it read. That was the moment when I stopped taking those mental notes for my storytelling session with Diana.

I was marched past the truncated "lighthouse" to a long, rectangular one-story building. There was a small room at the entrance with a motel-style reception counter. The man who had fingerprinted me had come along and had a little whispering session with the man behind the counter. The guards stood by as the "receptionist" took me through the door, into an unfinished concrete hallway lined with metal doors, each with a square barred opening. There were 14 cells in all, seven on each side. He opened the second door on the right and immediately closed it behind me.

The cell was an arm's span in width and exactly twice the length. There were two bunk beds but there were two other men. One, in his teens, looked like an Arab and the other like a South Asian. The Arab teenager was leaning in the far corner, hands behind his back. He examined me, trying to judge whether he should speak to me and in what language. I looked Middle Eastern but my T-shirt threw him off. The corners of his mouth twitched with indecision, interrupted with flashes of a smile. The other cellmate was on the top bed, propped up on his elbows, smiling at me, his broad muscular shoulders cradling a pockmarked, shaven head.

When the teenager moved out of the corner I became a bit guarded—despite his pleasant demeanor—because his hands were still behind his back. He was scanning me, from T-shirt to face. Noticing my caution, he shifted his hands to one side to show me that he was cuffed. Then he greeted me with a Marhaba, guessing right. I answered him and then greeted the man on the bed in English. He did not answer but sustained his smile. The teenager did his best to approximate the Lebanese colloquial, asking my name and my father's. Here we go again.

"Lebanese?"

"Yes."

"Shi'i, right?"

"Yes. How did you know?"

"From your father's name."

"Really? Not from the family name? Our family is a well-known Shi'i family from south Lebanon."

"There are El-Amines all over. I am Ali." He turned and offered his cuffed hands for me to shake. "Have a seat," Ali said as if I had come over for tea. "Welcome."

I sat on the lower bunk, its sponge mattress barely covered with a gray sheet. Ali sat a comfortable distance away, resting his back against the wall. He asked me why I was arrested and I answered that I was not sure. I told him my story and he told me his. He had been picked up in front of his neighborhood mosque for distributing "political" fliers after Friday prayers. He paused in reflection and then he said that something was happening out there. There had been an influx of new prisoners in the past two days. The government was nervous about something. I told him I didn't expect to be there long, though I did not reveal my father's association with the US military. He smiled and said that he also had thought he would be out in a day or two.

"And how long have you been here?" I asked.

"Six months," he said. My face flushed and I felt sweat bead around my temples and the tip of my nose.

"Like this?" I pointed to his handcuffs.

"Yes, like this." He noticed the sudden change in my disposition and hurried to say that some people leave much sooner. He knew someone who left yesterday and had been there for less than a month. That did not help.

"The fact that they didn't run you through the tower first means that they are not sure about you," Ali said.

"The tower?"

"Yes, that little building outside in the clearing. That's where they initiate the prisoners. They obviously did not interrogate you there."

"But they did interrogate me in the office," I replied.

"No, they did not interrogate you," he searched my face to make sure he had not missed anything, and said it again. I sat on the ground, away from the grimy bed, and kneaded my OP shorts with sweaty palms.

Time slowed down; the sun took forever to set. A red haze hung in the cell for the longest hour. Then in a moment, it diminished, leaving us in the dreariness of a bare light bulb and bare concrete. Despair set it in.

There was a long silence interrupted by prisoners mumbling their evening prayers. I heard the main door open. Ali had just finished his prayers, which he performed on the floor, hands behind his back. He told me that they were about to serve dinner and that I would not be able to eat it. But not to worry, he assured me, he would scrounge up something for me this first night. I felt a bit insulted, thinking of the worm-infested olives that were the centerpiece of every meal at my old school. "I will be ok, I was conditioned to eat lousy food in boarding school," I assured him. Ali smiled kindly, saying nothing.

There was a loud knock on the metal door, as if we could open it, and then the door swung in with a whine. A cauldron was wheeled into view. A man in a dark green jumpsuit, looking more like a mechanic than a cook, accompanied another in a white thobe and headdress. Ali gave them his back. The man with the thobe unlocked his handcuffs and handed each of us a wooden bowl. Ali and the South Asian stood in the doorway, holding out bowls like Dickensian characters, and I followed suit. The foam-ringed cauldron brimmed with a greasy orange film. The server began to stir the swill underneath until it turned a light brown. He ladled the blend into our bowls. We were handed two pieces of pita bread as hard as Frisbees, then the door slammed shut. Ali slid down against the wall and sat on the ground. He set his bowl down, rubbed his wrists, and proceeded to stir the alleged soup, slurping it up before it separated again, taking bites from the hard bread in between. I remained standing, looking down at my bowl, watching the grease separate again and float on the surface. The liquid was lukewarm and gave off a scent of something inorganic, something petroleum-based. Ali advised me to drink it, knowing well that I was not going to. He tilted his bowl to down the last bits, a sight that turned my stomach. He took the bowl out of my hands and gave it to our cellmate, who dipped the petrified bread into the broth and gulped down the mush.

The guard opened our cell again to put the cuffs on Ali. Ali waited a few minutes, then put his ear to the bars and listened until he heard the hallway door close. He asked me to stand with my back against the door. He approached me until we were nose to nose and asked me to cup my hands so that he could step up to the vent above the door. Ali was light and I lifted him easily to the vent. He managed to balance himself, despite the handcuffs, and set his chin down on the bottom of the opening.

"Brothers!" he yelled into the void. "Brothers, we have a new prisoner. His name is Zein Mohammad Bakir El-Amine, a Shi'i!"

What came back was a discord of shouts that turned into a harmonized chant. I could not tell if it was a show of solidarity or indignation. As the noise died down, Ali spoke into the makeshift intercom, "Samir, can you send something for our brother to eat?"

There was a faint response from a cell on the other end of the hall. Ali jumped down and asked me to watch the barred window in the door. I stood there for about ten minutes and then I heard Muhammad, Abdallah, Yusuf, and other names being called out, each time from a different cell, by a different person. Six names were called in all, each sounding closer and closer. Then I heard, "Zein, Zein El-Amine," and saw a string swing across my vision, with a small shiny object attached. "Grab it!" Ali repeated as I jumped back, startled. I managed to hook the item with my index finger and reel it in. It was a wedge of cheese, in the familiar aluminum foil wrapping with the iconic picture of the laughing cow, indented at the center from the string. I was about to step back when I heard the names being called again and saw another piece of string swing across the opening, this time with a piece of bread attached. The names called again, ending with mine and followed by the appearance of another string, this one carrying a small egg. I was overwhelmed—seven hungry men had passed the food to me. I sat on the bed, gathered all the goodies in my palms, smothered the cheese across the piece of soft pita bread, and wolfed it down. Then I grasped the egg. It looked too small to be a chicken egg but it didn't matter. The South Asian man, probably a Pakistani, was peering at me from the top bunk. I was about to crack the egg against the bedpost but Ali yelled at me to stop. The egg was raw, he said, for nourishment and not for taste. I had to puncture the top and suck out the yolk. I said I would gag. So he told me to set it aside for later.

After dinner Ali and I sat across from each other talking. He was leaning back on the bed, trying to get as comfortable as possible with bound hands. I was leaning against the wall, feeling sluggish and nauseated. Someone was singing across the way. A couple of hours passed, and then I heard the hallway door open. I was sure they had found out who I was and were coming to get me. Our cell door opened and my heart leaped in anticipation. A man with a white thobe and headdress followed by a uniformed soldier walked between Ali and me and started shouting at the other prisoner. "Why are you looking out of the window?" The Pakistani backed up in the corner on the upper bunk, as if anticipating a beating. The official told him that next time they would take him to the tower. *Al-Burj! Al-Burj!* I saw the tear-rimmed fear in the prisoner's eyes. He must not have understood it was a warning. He must have thought they were taking him to the tower right then and there.

Just as quickly, the official charged out and the Pakistani fell back in tears. Ali tried to explain to him with hand gestures that he was not going to the tower. The Pakistani nodded. Ali patted him on the shoulder with his forehead, the closest thing to a comforting touch he could offer, then listened at the door again. We heard a metal door shut, then another. Ali sat in front of me. He turned his back to me and asked me to hold the cuffs down on the ground. I did. He moved his ass above the cuffs and wriggled his way out. He was still handcuffed but at least his hands were now in front of him.

I asked what had just happened. "They thought that he was looking out of the window and they were about to beat him up. But I think that they realized that they got the wrong cell."

"So what if he looks out of the window?"

"There must have been a dignitary visiting. There is definitely something going on. High officials do not visit during the night. Somebody is nervous."

Ali took advantage of his liberated hands to perform the night prayer. I was at a moment in my life where I was becoming jaded about religion, for my fellow Lebanese had been killing each other in its name. But seeing a chained man pray allowed no room for cynicism. I watched him as he inadvertently muzzled himself every time he brought up his hands to his temples. Prayer had never seemed more meditative, more purposeful.

"Are you getting sleepy?" he asked. I answered no. I was holding out hope that I would be released before dawn. Surely my father would soon get a call in Dhahran and he would call the American general, and the general in turn would call the American ambassador in Manama, and then some apologetic Bahraini official would arrive to reprimand the people who put me here. I imagined sleeping until noon, another nice breakfast, and playing tennis in my baby blue OP shorts. Then later Diana and I would go to the Anchor Inn, and she would order her pint of Double Diamond and I would order a double scotch with coke, and we would get sloshed by the pool and laugh about this whole episode.

"You should sleep," said Ali. "They'll wake us up at dawn for tea and bread. You should eat in the morning. It is the only thing you're going to be able to eat because it is just tea and bread." I told him that I was going to stay up but did not betray my optimism.

"You should sleep on the bed and I will sleep on the ground here."

"What? No, no, that is not right."

"I don't sleep much. I have to get my hands back behind my back now. I am just as uncomfortable on the floor as I am on the bed." He set his fists on the floor. "Here help me get back in position. I can't be caught like this."

I held down the cuffs and he moved back into his original position. He moved to the corner and rested his head against the wall. "Don't worry. This is normal for me. Believe me, it makes no difference."

I was very hesitant about lying down on the bed. There was no pillowcase or top sheet, and I worried about bugs. Most importantly, it would be to surrender to the knowledge that no one was coming for me that night. I slowly examined the bed in the snatches of moonlight, looking for telltale scurrying. I brushed off the pillow and laid my OP shorts on top of it. The Asian man was already in deep sleep and Ali was watching me intermittently between moments of rest. My ankles began to itch, as did my head. I spent the night popping up in bed and swatting at the invisible.

I snatched what felt like a half-hour of sleep before there was a clunking at the door. Someone was banging a tin cup and yelling. As long as I had lived on the Arabian Peninsula, I still could not understand the Gulf dialect when it was spoken at a casual pace. Ali told me to wake up. "Be ready or they will pass you by."

I saw no ray of light, but there was no way to confirm the time. Ali stood in front of the door. When they flung it open, he turned his back to them and a man in a sort of gray jumpsuit, pant legs rolled up as if he had just done his ablutions, pulled a steaming pot into view while a Bahraini man in civilian clothes moved in, jangling his keys, and unlocked the handcuffs. It was Smiley from the processing office. As Smiley moved out, the man in the jumpsuit moved in with enamel-covered tin cups, chipped and rusted on the rims. The Asian eagerly extended his arm. The three of us stood side by side, cups extended, as the man scooped the hot liquid from the big pot. Then another man, who had been clanking on the metal doors of the cells, came in with a stack of flatbread. The bread was again Frisbee-like in rigidity but my cellmates grabbed it and were munching on it even before they settled in their little corners. From the smell coming off the light brown brew, I guessed it was tea and it must have had some milk in it. I later learned it was the best meal of the day. When we finished eating, Ali rushed to do the dawn prayer, again taking advantage of his free hands.

I asked Ali about the daily schedule. There was none—no exercise, no walks in the yard.

I asked about the bathroom. "They let us out in the morning. It should be soon, so be ready because you have five minutes to do your business. Then there is another time in the afternoon. And then there is this." He pointed to a pot that I had somehow missed in the corner next to the door. Ali said, "Don't look at it. I will empty it at the bathroom break." The south Asian man laughed.

"Does he understand Arabic?" I asked.

"A little. He's Pakistani. He was in the country with a counterfeit passport or he was making counterfeit passports. I don't know. He is not a political prisoner, and they did not take him through the tower."

"What is the tower?

Ali regarded me warily, weighing what he should say. Then he averted his eyes and explained, "The tower is where they take you if you are arrested for political reasons. It is a narrow round structure with a sandpit for a floor. They seat you in a chair, blindfold you and tie your hands behind your back and then they start with the questions and the beatings. There are usually two of them and they take turns punching you in the face. They do this for hours and then they leave you bleeding and tied to the chair for days, without food, without water, without allowing you to go to the bathroom. You bleed, piss and shit yourself for days. Then they take you to the showers and bring you to your cell."

There came a knock for the bathroom break. There was shouting, a clanking of doors and slapping of flip-flops. When they opened our door, the Pakistani man ran past me. Ali, released from his handcuffs, also took off. So I raced after them. I heard a smattering of greetings as other prisoners passed me. One patted me on the shoulder and was reproached by the guard. I walked into a stall and took a piss, and rushed to the sink to wash my hands, only to realize that the powder I had spilled on my hands was laundry detergent. I stood there confused, as Ali tugged at my elbow. We ran out as the guards herded others in to take our place. Back in the cell, I sought my OP shorts to wipe my hands.

My daydreams of being set free were already spent by the second day. I started to remember things that had happened while I was in high school, signs that this happy island was troubled but that we were too engrossed in our navels or too stoned to notice. The morning rattle woke me from a dream about a neighborhood covered in long black banners and doppelgangers of Ali, in black shirts and pants, walking around passing out leaflets.

As I drank my tea and crunched my dry bread, I traced the dream back to an incident one sunny day when we were on a bus proceeding along the tree-lined boulevard, en route to school. The palms were swaying in the wind. The bus was abuzz about the previous night's "Muppet Show" episode, a weekly occurrence. The traffic was unusually heavy. As was my habit, I was sitting next to Mahdi, the driver, a Bahraini Shi'i barely 18. He cursed the traffic under his breath. He peeled onto a parallel single-lane road and then made a sharp turn taking us into a residential neighborhood. As he went deeper into the neighborhood, we noticed run-down buildings and open sewers. Then we entered another neighborhood packed with mid-rises, their balconies draped with long black banners that skirted the sidewalks and flapped in the breeze. We drove through this procession in total silence; you could hear the banners snapping. Then, just like that, we were back on the boulevard again, in the full sunlight and happy chatter of the daily commute.

In the first three days I learned more about Bahrain than I had in the three years I spent in the country previously. A rebellion had been brewing and it was being snuffed out before it spilled out of the restive suburbs into the squares of the capital. More answers about mysterious happenings that had punctuated my carefree days and disco nights: a close friend and I were eating lunch when we heard chants from an unseen approaching crowd. A policeman knocking with a stick on the storefronts. Merchants rolling down their metal doors with a loud rattle. Muffled shouts rising, falling, then dissolving into scattered wails. Half an hour later, the merchants opened back up. We walked out of the café to a scene of scattered flip-flops and the sting of smoke that hadn't settled. It was as if a crowd had been sucked up into a hovercraft that jetted off in silence, leaving nothing but their shoes. The incident had not troubled me until now, as I sat on my OP shorts, hair like a Brillo pad, scruff on my chin.

More silence, less talk. More listening to other prisoners. It seemed like every prisoner on the block was a Bahraini Shi'i except the guy at the far end. That man oozed resilience. He sang every morning and every evening. The morning songs were light-hearted, full of false hope, a sugar high that left you sick in its wake and made the silence all the more dreadful. The evening songs were mournful, the saddest of Umm Kulthum and Farid al-Atrash, songs that stuck in the throat.

It was day four and we had just finished our lunch. The guards came to collect our utensils and started barking orders that I did not understand. Our Pakistani cellmate ran past me motioning to his bristled head, making a lathering motion. Would we be allowed a shower? I saw that he had grabbed a cloth and so I snapped up my OP shorts and ran after him. In the corridor, a guard shouted at the prisoners, pushing them toward the bathroom. I saw men enter the shower stalls fully clothed and disrobe inside. I did the same and turned on the knob in the wall, dousing myself in cold water. In the soap dish, I found a plastic jug that had been cut in half and filled with powder. In my daze, I did not stop to consider if it might be the same laundry detergent I had mistakenly used before. I dumped some powder on my head and around my shoulders. The guards were already rushing our shift out, slapping the mildewed shower curtains. I dried myself as efficiently as I could with my shorts and got dressed. I found myself running through the corridor while trying to button up my pants and put my shirt on, remnants of the powder in my hair and on my body. The minute I got into the cell I began to itch all over.

Ali told me about his family. His father worked a menial job and was always away. His tales of his mother remind me of my aunts back in south Lebanon. I imagine her scarfed in black, doting on him, kissing him when he came home, when he sat down to eat, when he passed some final exam. I imagined her voice like my aunt's, full of sad tenderness. But Ali talked about his family in the past tense, never in the present, and certainly not in the future. It was a survival mechanism, I understood later. You could not hope. It was a surefire route to greater despair. You had to be immersed in the moment. Span the hours of the early morning, long for the tea and bread as if something to be savored. Then pass the hours between tea and lunch. Watch the light. Venture out in your mind, but not too far, maybe across the street from the fort. Walk back and forth in the cell. Set a goal, a number of "laps." Go beyond it to create a stimulus in a stagnant environment. Exhaust yourself before lunch so that you can nap. Look forward to a respite from the oppressive heat. Then dinner, then a couple of stories as if hanging out with friends. All the while, do not let the idea of escape or reunions come to you. Keep hope at bay.

On the fourth or the fifth day, the guards showed up at an unusual time. There were two of them and they came to our cell first. For a second I dared to hope again, but then I saw them release Ali's cuffs, and I saw that there were other guards opening other cells. I realized it was something else, perhaps another bathroom break. I grabbed my OP shorts, which had become my towel, handkerchief, pillowcase, and floormat. Ali had his usual look of resignation. We were herded out to a courtyard. There was a structure in the center that gave the impression of being a fountain. Orders were given that I could not hear but I saw that the prisoners had started to converge around the fountain. It was drab unfinished concrete and there was a stub of a tiled column in the center with two faucets. Men started washing up and filling their cups with water. I walked slowly because I felt something that I had not felt for days—the sun. I subconsciously closed my eyes and opened them to see other prisoners looking at me. It was the first time that I had a chance to really see my fellow inmates. They all looked Bahraini to me except one tall man with a pale complexion and light brown hair, who I took to be Syrian. They all looked so confident, so purposeful. I expected a zombified horde but what I saw was resilience. I wished for that strength.

Day six. It was mid-morning and unusually hot. Ali was more chatty than he had ever been with me. Our Pakistani cellmate— for the first time—was trying to figure out what we were talking about. Ali's hands were not cuffed; I had helped him do his miraculous maneuver earlier when the guards cleared. He was no longer talking to me as a cellmate but as a friend, one who would be there with him for a long time. I was too much in the moment to be depressed about that prospect. We heard a rattle at the main door and I scrambled to help Ali slip into his cuffed position. The guards were moving so fast that Ali had barely got into position when the door opened.

"Zein El-Amine," said a man in civilian clothes flanked by two men in military garb. I couldn't speak so I raised my hand. "Gather your things," he said.

My things? I picked up my OP shorts and turned to Ali to get a hint of what was happening. I saw a slight, skewed smile and one eye brimming with tears. He quickly approached and I moved to hug him, his chest bumping mine. "You're going home," he said. And then louder as I moved away, "Send my regards to your mother."

When the outside door opened, the sun hit me with the force of an explosion. I winced, put up a hand up to my forehead, and kept trotting. Everything was in pieces: one second I was in the cell, the next I was in the sunshine, and then I was in a car speeding down a highway, flanked by two guards. I am not sure how fast they were driving but it felt like hyperspace.

Back home that same day, amidst family and visiting friends, I heard one woman tell another, "Thank God. They almost killed her."

My father confirmed it. "Yes, they almost did kill your mother. They told us there was an attempted coup on the day you arrived in Bahrain and that there were Saudi Arabia Shi'a involved. Those men happened to be on the same plane as you. They said you were involved in the coup and that they were starting to 'disappear' those involved." Rumor had it that they were taking prisoners to the desert, executing them, and claiming no knowledge of their existence. "That news knocked your mom flat. She has been bed-ridden for days."

I am tempted to say that I did not sleep that night; that I kept on waking up swatting imaginary cockroaches and scratching non-existent fleas; that I had dreams of the tower, of being bound and blindfolded, my head a bloody pulp. But no, I went to the small bedroom of my childhood, I laid in one of the two twin beds and fell into a deep sleep, a sleep free of fear, free of trauma, with dreams of ordinary things. I would like to pretend that I woke up snatching at the air, not knowing where I was, thinking I was back in the cell, looking around to see Ali on the floor, his back against the wall so as not to strain his shoulders. But no, I woke up knowing exactly where I was. The only thing that I kept on that day was the scraggly beard that I had grown during my imprisonment.

I can't remember where my mom was that morning, though. I assume she stayed in bed another day. She is missing from the memory of my first day back completely. Maybe she is missing because I erased her from that day. Maybe she is missing because she fell ill months later and died within a year of that day, from lung cancer, at the age of 53. Maybe that day was what connected her death with my imprisonment. Maybe I want to sever that connection. Maybe I do not want that child with his OP shorts, ignorant of the consequences of his actions and sleepwalking through his youth, to take any responsibility for the disintegration that ended the life of the person he loved the most and who loved him the most. Maybe the anger that simmers under my surface today, that constant roil, started on the day where I connected the deeds of that murderous government with my personal tragedy. They whittled away at her until she was gone. Maybe that day is the day I lost any measure of healthy fear.

I got some more clarifications from US officers who knew my father: The housing complex that I cut across belonged to the Bahraini minister of interior. The timing of my accidental trespass was very bad—a day after an attempted coup against the ruling family. The accused in the coup attempt were Shi'a. Some of the Saudi Arabians accused of helping them had indeed traveled to Bahrain on my flight. The day before my arrival, the government had discovered a warehouse full of new Bahraini military uniforms, accurate to the T with the exception of the buttons, which were marked "Made in Iran." But even if I had picked up a paper or listened to the news, I would not have known, for there was a total media blackout. The military and secret police were arresting any Shi'i man who was not where he was supposed to be. A young man trespassing on the property of the minister of interior was easily thought to be a "suspected terrorist."

I would like to conclude that I was still fuming after my debriefing, but no. I walked out into that December Arabian sun and felt my blood ululate in its nourishment. I went to the base exchange, its shelves fully stocked and bathed in fluorescent light. I picked out some soap, watched the people eyeing my scruffy appearance, and enjoyed their discomfort.

The Birds of Achrafieh

⸻

IT WAS A WEDNESDAY NIGHT, WHICH MEANT THAT IT WAS *Six Million Dollar Man* night, and a dozen boys and girls, left behind at the Good Shepherd School were fighting over what to watch on TV. The TV, which belonged to one of the boys on the third floor of the dormitory, had been moved to the vacated second floor in order to allow the few girls left in the dorm to watch it with the boys. The girls, who ranged in age from eleven to fourteen, wanted to watch the last episode of the soap opera Rabii, and the boys, all of the same age of twelve, wanted to watch Steve Austin's latest adventures, as they had done every week for the past six months. When the argument turned into a pillow fight Fatima, the dorm counselor, shut off the TV and sent everybody to bed. So the kids left, moaning and groaning all the way through their nightly regime of changing into their pajamas, folding their clothes at the foot of the bed, and brushing their teeth. They knew quite well that Fatima was going to roll the TV into her room and watch Rabii with the girls, as she had done every week.

The girls' room upstairs had ten beds—five on each side with metal, built-in lockers between them, and three tall windows that faced the school courtyard and the valley below. Rana's bed was the one closest to the windows. As she lay down on her side, she faced the starry sky above the valley. The shooting started as she was dozing off, first like the poppings of a firecracker, then the sounds thickened and the exchange sounded as if it came from one source. When the fighting died away two hours later, Rana started to doze off again. Her eyelids gathered the last light of her waking hours—— the inclined ascent of tracer bullets filling up her window, streaking her patch of the night like shooting stars returning to their point of origin, lulling her to sleep with their sporadic crackles.

Mustapha woke up to the same sight he had been waking up to for the past three weeks of the fighting—bed springs. He was under his bed staring at the spiraling metal. His first reflex each morning used to be to push against this wire mesh—overwhelmed by his first conscious thought of being netted or imprisoned. But now the gunfire had become his alarm clock and this cage of springs, his security blanket. He had recently started to count the springs, just as some count sheep, to deal with the trauma of the early morning gunfire. He already knew that there were 60, but he would count them, starting from the left-hand top corner spring going across to the bottom right-hand corner spring at the foot of the bed. After he had accounted for all of the springs he would come out carefully from under the bed. He was being extra careful today. He was thinking about his encounter the night before with Michel. Michel was the only senior who had remained in the school after it had been evacuated. He had come upon Mustapha and his friends, Ali and Jaguar, as they played marbles in the underground parking garage of the administrative building. He asked them what their names were, what families they came from, and why they weren't able to get them out of the dormitory when the school shut down. When they didn't pay him any attention, he stepped on their marbles and told them to look up when he talked to them. Then he asked Mustapha if he was Palestinian, and Mustapha answered yes. Michel then smacked him on the back of his neck so hard that his head almost hit the ground. The startled Mustapha looked up, rubbing his neck, face contorted with pain. "What is your story? What did I do to you?" he cried.

"You came here," was Michel's answer.

Mustapha got dressed in his empty room. Ali and Jaguar slept in the room next door. Jaguar was really George, but they all called him Jaguar because he was obsessed with toy cars and made a vrr-rooooommm vroom sound when he ran. He had been separated from them two days ago when Fatima discovered that he had head lice. She had turned him over her lap above a basin filled with kerosene and picked out the lice one by one. She pinched each little insect between her fingers and rinsed her hand with the kerosene. Every time that Mustapha tried to free his head from her grasp she pushed it back down and slapped him on his back. "You better not tell your parents about this when they come for you," she kept saying. He didn't want to tell her that his parents already knew about it because he had head lice for as long as he could remember. His grandmother once told him that there have been lice in the family since 1948. That's why he thought it was silly for Fatima to separate him from the other kids. He had been sleeping in the same room with Ali and Jaguar for the past six months, and they never had head lice even though they bathed less thoroughly than he did. He knew their bathing habits because Mr. Louka, the boys' dorm counselor, used to make them shower in pairs so that they could all be finished before bedtime.

Fatima would have never known about the lice if she hadn't overheard Ali telling Jaguar that Mustapha has "shiny little spiders" crawling in his hair. Mustapha had sworn, as his head was being held over the floating dead lice, that he would choke the breath out of Ali as soon as Fatima freed him. But when Mustapha had found Ali he took one look at his stick-figure body and that dispro-portionately large cone head of his and figured that if he got him in a headlock he would probably decapitate him. So he just gave Ali a little shove, which set his head off-balance, and Ali fell back folding at the knees because his feet were pinned in place by his oversized, corrective shoes.

Mustapha rolled out from under the bed and walked around the boys to the next room without acknowledging them. He changed into his blue polyester shorts and white shirt with the Brazilian flag that he saved for soccer games. The boys marveled, as always, at the size of his thighs and his shoulder muscles. His darkly-hued body lacked definition, but it had the solidity and texture of hardened clay.

"They came for you last night but Ali and I fought them off," Jaguar said. Mustapha ignored him. "They came at midnight asking for you," Jaguar went on, "they said 'Where is the Palestinian?' and I said 'What Palestinian?' They said 'Mustapha Al Ghalayini.' I said 'There's no Mustapha here.' Then I told them that there was something moving under my bed, and when they set their Kalishnikovs on the floor to look under my bed, Haa!" Jaguar knelt on one knee and sliced the air with several karate chops.

Mustapha finished putting on his shoes, and he stomped his foot towards Jaguar, feigning an attack. Jaguar jumped back and crouched in a karate stance that he had learned from Bruce Lee movies. Mustapha walked up to him and got him in a headlock and they started rolling on the bed.

That same morning, Rana woke up to the sound of sporadic machine-gun fire. She turned from her side to her back and stared at the ceiling listening for another spurt. Nothing happened. She looked around at the lined beds and saw that Naseem was also awake and listening intently. Rana checked the time; it was 8:30. "Good," she thought, "the school buses can't go out now." She had learned by now that if the buses do not leave the school by 8:00 then that would mean another day off.

The shooting started again, this time a little closer. The crackling continued for 15 minutes before it stopped. "That should do it," she thought. She raised her head and smiled at Naseem, who smiled back. They turned onto their sides in unison and went back to sleep as the gunfire continued.

She didn't wake up again until 10:00 am. It was quiet outside, and Naseem was already dressed and organizing her locker. "Did you go for breakfast?" asked Rana as she stretched out.

"Yes," replied Naseem.

"Fried zucchini and eggs again?" asked Rana, wrinkling her nose in disgust.

"Yes," Naseem answered.

The school had been closed for three weeks because of the fighting between the Phalangists, whose headquarters were located uphill from the school, in Achrafieh, and the Palestinians based in Tel Al Zaatar refugee camp downhill from the school. Since the dormitory kitchen was not stocked for emergencies, the school principal asked the Phalangists to bring in some food supplies. The Phalangists had intercepted a truck transporting zucchini the day before and had arrested the driver because they suspected that he was taking food supplies to Tel Al Zaatar. Thus the dormitory kitchen was stocked with enough zucchini to feed the trapped dorm students for a month. Fatima, who had to cook for the students, tried to be creative with the few staples she had available. She fried the zucchini with eggs and served it for breakfast. She stuffed it with rice on another day and served it for lunch. She fried it with onions and tomatoes for dinner. And when she ran out of recipes she served one of her zucchini combinations at a different time of the day so, for example, the kids would find the egg-zucchini dish being served for dinner one evening, fried zucchini with onions and tomatoes for breakfast, and so on

Rana changed without washing her face or brushing her teeth. She patted down her short, thick black hair that was bunched up to one side from sleep. She walked up to Naseem pretending to be modeling. "How do I look?" she asked Naseem while pushing up her hair from behind.

Naseem looked up at Rana. "Pretty, very pretty" she said sarcastically.

"I knew you would approve," Rana said, fluttering her eyelashes. Naseem was envious of Rana because even with her unkempt hair and the oversized boys' shirts that she always wore, she still looked adorable. On a school outing to the Rouche the month before, a couple of the dorm students stood in line along the boardwalk to have their fortunes told. When it was Rana's turn, the Gypsy looked at Rana's face with its porcelain-pure skin and the intelligent jewel-brown eyes and told her, "I feel sorry for the men in your life.

If they get through the thicket of your lashes they'll be entangled in the honeywebs of your eyes." Then the Gypsy smiled proudly, baring her gold teeth, and proceeded to use the same line on all the girls that followed Rana.

Rana looked out of one of the three tall windows in the big room. From there, she could see the vast concrete courtyard below which was bordered by the dormitory and the school administration building. A wide set of steps connected this large courtyard with a smaller one below it. All along the outside borders of the lower courtyard was a high masonry wall with a wrought-iron gate through which the school buses entered to park under the high school building. The gate was now blocked by the Phalangists who had built a barricade made of a combination of sandbags and brand new refrigerators looted from a nearby appliance store. At the farthest corner of the perimeter wall there was a taxicab with smashed windows and a crunched fender. The driver had been shot the week before when he didn't stop at the barricade, and he crashed into the courtyard wall. Although the students had seen some intense fighting in the past three weeks, that was the first killing that they had witnessed.

Rana spotted her sister Suha sitting on a concrete bench beside Michel. Michel's left hand was bandaged. He had been telling everyone how he got wounded in a gunfight that he claimed he was involved in yesterday. From the looks of it, Rana was sure that he was trying to get Suha's sympathies. He put his good hand around her shoulders and Suha looked at him with admiration. Rana considered spitting on Michel from the window but decided against it. He would never dare touch Suha if the school was still in session. The gunfight that he had been bragging about was between the Phalangists and a Palestinian fighter who had positioned himself atop the church across the street. At first the Phalangists were shooting at the Palestinian from the streets. Then they decided to go into the school and get on top of the dormitory building to get a better shot at him. The girls' floor is the topmost floor of the building so they were awakened by the sound of boots stomping above them followed by machine-gun fire that sounded as if it was coming from the girls' room itself. Panicked and confused, the girls ran down to the boys' floor and jumped into the beds of the frightened boys. The gunfight lasted about fifteen minutes after which the girls opened their eyes to find themselves face-to-face with the boys: some looking startled, some smiling in disbelief.

Today was an early spring day, and so the field across the street from the lower courtyard was filled with daisies. The morning sun rendered the field shadowless, making it difficult for Rana to look directly at it.

"I don't think that there'll be any shooting today," she told Naseem as she inhaled the chill morning breeze.

"Why do you say that?" asked Naseem.

"Because nobody could possibly be in the mood to kill anyone on a day like this. Besides, look at the birds in the pine trees over there. They're singing and feeding and flying and singing all over the place," said Rana melodiously.

"What do the birds have to do with it?" asked Naseem.

"They know what's going on. They know what a gun looks like. They even remember the faces of the hunters that come into their areas. When I used to go with my grandfather to our olive grove, the nearest bird would be a kilometer away. But whenever I went with my mother there'd be so many birds that we would be afraid to sit under a tree," explained Rana. When she turned to look out of the window again, she spotted the boys getting ready to play soccer.

Usually, on a Thursday morning, the boys would be quietly filing out of their rooms into the dark, cold hallway that leads to the bathrooms. They would wash their faces and brush their teeth at the row of sinks that lined both sides of the washroom. Then they would have to change, make up their beds, and organize their lockers. After all their chores were done Mr. Louka would blow his whistle signaling the daily inspection. The boys would stand in attention in front of their beds with their hands extended. Mr. Louka would then walk between the boys, slapping a wooden ruler on the palm of his hand. If he saw something he didn't like—an improperly tucked corner of a bed, a long fingernail, or dirt in the corner of an eye—he would pass the guilty party and then he would suddenly turn and smack the boy's knuckles with the ruler. What frightened the boys more is when Mr. Louka walked through without his ruler. On those days, he would fiddle with his ring, which had a large maroon-colored stone. He would watch his biceps ripple and strain against his rolled-up sleeve as he turned the ring around his middle finger. Then, he would approach his victim and pat him on the back, and with a swift upward movement of his hand, he would move the stone along the boy's spine and rap the back of his skull with it.

Earlier this morning, Ali had been startled out of his sleep with the thought of Mr. Louka returning. But he quickly got his bearings and pondered on his good fortune. The school was closed. Mr. Louka was gone. Rana's parents weren't able to get her before the roads were closed. And that boy Sameer, who Rana liked, was out on a weekend visit with his uncle when the fighting broke out. "Thank you, God, of the universe," he murmured mockingly to himself before jumping out of bed fully dressed for the soccer game.

Jaguar woke up at least an hour before everyone else. He washed, brushed his teeth, and dressed out of habit. He was playing with his cars, making the low motor revving sound that earned him his nickname. The tips of his ears were curved down, something he claimed to be an aerodynamic feature rather than a mutation from birth. He was trying to be considerate, revving up his cars quietly and driving them up hilly pillows and across linoleum deserts in a hushed manner that made him sound like a happy cat. Most of his close friends were gone but at least Ali and Mustapha were stuck with him. He always wanted to play with them but he had to do it in secret when school was in session because his friends looked down on them. They called Ali a "dirty peasant" and made fun of his southern dialect. They would point to an object and ask Ali to name it. Ali would name it, with his southern Lebanese drawl, and they would laugh and parrot him all day. With Mustapha, all the insults and taunts were always behind his back because they were afraid of him.

Now he didn't have to sneak around to be with Mustapha and Ali. He can motor all over the school with them—in the courtyards, the classrooms, down all the hallways. No one can stop him or make him crash—not teachers, no counselors, and no stuffy rich friends.

"You've got to see this. The three stooges are playing on the same team." Rana was now yelling to Naseem, her husky voice breaking into a high pitch. Naseem joined her at the window, and they broke out into a giggle. Ali was playing defense, shifting from side to side, and dragging his orthopedic shoes on the concrete. His arms were stretched out and his upper body bent forward in anticipation. His large hooked nose stuck out in front of him as if he was sniffing his opponents. His closely cropped hair was cut in Frankenstein fashion: straight across the middle of his brow and straight down along his temples. From where Rana and Naseem stood, Ali resembled, in both awkwardness and appearance, a newly hatched eaglet.

Unlike Ali, Mustapha didn't seem too excited about the game. He stood between the two cinder blocks that marked the goal, feet apart and his hands on hips. He had squared shoulders with a short, wide neck that supported a disproportionately small head. He had dark blemishes on his cheeks and on his arms. The scars were the result of Mustapha's many past, brave attempts to block the ball. He had been playing goalie at least every other day for the past six months, and he had yet to block one ball from entering the goal. Jaguar was running with the ball into the other team's half-court. He ran towards the players, chin to chest, like a charging bull and making car engine sounds. "Vrrrrrrrr!"

He passed the first player and motored towards the goal only to realize that he didn't have the ball. He looked back just in time to watch the defensive player from the opposing team go through Ali, bypassing the ball between Ali's anchored feet and kick the ball towards Mustapha. In a split second, Mustapha sprung out of his statue-like stance and flew sideways to block the ball. At the point when Mustapha was perfectly parallel with the concrete ground, the ball bounced off of his face and rebounded off the charging player's chest and into the goal. Mustapha fell on the hard ground and recoiled to a fetal position. Ali ran up to him and asked if he was OK. "I am alright, just let me catch my breath," whispered Mustapha. A minute later, Mustapha was up again, standing in his usual pose–hands on the hips, legs spread, watching the ball with an expressionless face.

Rana and Naseem suffered a laughing fit that was triggered by Jaguar's quixotic charge and sustained by Ali's defense play and Mustapha's failed block. Ali spotted the girls at the window and began to point frantically at the gate near him. "What's he doing?" asked Naseem.

"I don't know," answered Rana, extending her head to get a better view of the gate.

"What is it?" asked Rana as she turned her palms up to indicate to Ali that she didn't know what he was trying to tell her. Ali pointed to himself and then to the field.

"The daisies? OK, OK." Rana said, nodding her head in an exaggerated manner.

"What is it?" asked Naseem.

"Last night when we were playing hide and seek, I hid with Ali under a school bus, and I started talking about all the things I used to do during spring break. I told him that we used to pick daisies and string them together to make necklaces—we used to do it with tobacco string and needles to imitate the way my aunt threads tobacco. So Ali told me that he was going to go out in the morning and pick me some daisies from the field. So I said OK."

"You said OK!" exclaimed Naseem.

"Oh, he won't do it. He won't be able to get past the Phalangists," Rana said confidently.

"I don't know. That boy is crazy. Look at him," said Naseem, pointing at the courtyard.

Ali was pretending to run in slow motion. He was imitating his favorite bionic superhero.

"I think he's funny," said Rana.

"Don't tell me that you're starting to like him," said Naseem, turning to face Rana.

Rana kept looking out of the window. "He kind of grows on you" she said, then she shouted, "Look, he actually intercepted the ball!"

Ali was heading toward the goal. He was wide open with the ball. Suddenly he stopped, took two steps back, and kicked the ball over the corner of the masonry wall—way right of the goal. The ball arched over the street, between the crashed cab and the militiamen, and fell into the field. He walked over to the makeshift goal and picked up the cinder blocks one at a time and placed them longways on top of each other. With a boost from Mustapha, he managed to climb on top of the blocks and pull himself over the wall. He straddled the wall, keeping his head down, like a jockey. The top of the wall was usually embedded with broken pieces of glass to discourage the dormitory students from escaping, but Ali had checked the corner the day before and he knew that it was the only area free of glass.

"No, no, you idiot! What are you doing?" Rana whispered through her teeth as she waved her arms frantically to get his attention.

"He's crazy," Naseem muttered as if hypnotized by the scene.

Ali looked below him at the crumpled hood of the shot-up taxi-cab. He slid down slowly, leaving his thin, rubber-like legs to the mercy of his heavy shoes. Fortunately, his shoes scraped the hood of the car, dissipating their pendulous momentum. He lay flat on the hood and watched the militiamen through the bullet-ridden windshield of the car. The men were sitting on two armchairs with their backs turned to him. Ali crawled backward over the bulky hood of the Mercedes, his eyes fixed on the men. He crossed the street moving his feet quietly from heel to toe with every step. As soon as he reached the edge of the field, he got on his hands and knees and crawled through the daisy patch. Rana smiled nervously because she noticed that Ali's yellow and white striped shirt blended perfectly with the wildflowers and wondered whether he had planned it that way. From her vantage point, she saw Ali's pointed head moving through the sea of flowers like a shark's fin. Suddenly the head stopped and Ali bolted straight up swiping at his left ear with one hand and at the air with the other. Then he started running swiftly in a crouched position back to the school wall, setting to flight hundreds of dandelion seeds that marked the path behind him. Mustapha, who was standing on the cinder blocks, had never seen Ali move so gracefully. Ali tiptoed across the road, his feet barely skimming the surface of the pavement. He paused for a second in front of the car and, seeing that the men hadn't noticed him, jumped to grab Mustapha's arm. But his grip wasn't strong enough, and he fell back on the hood of the car with a loud thud. The militiamen turned around and pulled their handguns out of their holsters.

"What are you doing?" asked one of the militiamen, motioning at Mustapha with the gun.

"We just wanted to get the ball from that field," Mustapha answered calmly, ignoring Ali's whispered pleas to keep quiet.

One of the men walked up to Ali and picked him up by the collar of his shirt.

"One second!" he yelled at the boy as he shook him back and forth, "one more second and you would've been sharing the taxi with Abu Aamar!" And with that, he pushed Ali's face against the back window of the car, but Ali put up his hands over his face and shut his eyes just in case the decomposed body of the driver was indeed left in the back seat. The militiaman then jerked him around and called to Mustapha, "Here, take your friend. I'll get your ball for you." The man lifted the boy at the waist and Mustapha pulled him over the wall. Then he waded through the field, located the ball, and, instead of giving it back to the kids, he threw it into the valley below. He waved his arms in the air and yelled, "Fucking bees!" as he walked back to join his friend. He nodded towards Mustapha who had remained standing on the cinder blocks, staring blankly at the armed man.

"Can I be of further assistance?" the man asked sarcastically.

"Yes, can you pick me some flowers?" answered Mustapha defiantly.

"Why are you getting ready for your funeral, you brother of a bitch?" the man yelled and drew his gun, causing Mustapha to jump back and fall off the blocks. He rolled the gun around his index finger and dropped it into his holster. His friend put his arm around the cowboy and shouted out to the neighborhood, "Eastwood can lick my ass. You're the best in the West!" They laughed and patted each other on the back as they walked back to the barricade.

Rana and Naseem ran down to see what had happened. But before they could get down to the first floor, they saw Michel chasing Suha, Rana's older sister up the stairs. He caught her right at the landing. At first, the girls thought that Suha was screaming for help but when Michel grabbed her around the waist and spun her around, they saw that she was laughing. Suha wriggled, pretending that she was trying to free herself. After a few minutes of this fake struggle, they both got quiet and breathy. Michel started lifting her from behind and dropping her, thrusting his pelvis against her with every jerk. At that moment Rana decided to put an end to this and stomped down the stairs, startling the couple. Suha brushed her long brown hair with her hands and, after exchanging dirty looks with Rana, she turned and slapped Michel on the hand and walked upstairs. Michel stood there, red-faced, adjusting his pants. He was wearing wide bell-bottomed jeans that were wrapped so tight around his torso that you could see the outline of his hip bones. Rana saw the bulge that extended from his groin to his pocket, and it scared her. He didn't bother to hide his erection from the girls. Rather he just hooked his thumbs into his pockets and leaned back against the wall as the girls passed him.

When the girls walked out into the courtyard, they saw the boys at the bottom of the staircase. Mustapha and Jaguar were sitting on both sides of Ali. Mustapha was looking closely at Ali's ear.

"What happened?" Rana exhorted as she came down the stairs.

"A bee stung him," Jaguar answered.

Ali quickly pulled up his yellow shirt and started wiping his face. Rana realized that he had been crying so she slowed down so as not to embarrass him.

"That's it," said Mustapha, pinching Ali's ear lobe. "See." he extended his index finger to show Ali the thorn-like object with the tiny moist strand that he just removed.

"It had a lot of guts," Jaguar said, smiling at Ali in an attempt to cheer him up.

Rana walked around to face them and saw that Ali's earlobe was red and swollen. It looked like he was wearing an earring. His face was tear-stained and the front of his shirt was smudged with pollen. The corners of his mouth twitched as he tried to straighten his frown. She examined his ear closely and then pulled him up by his hand.

"Come," she said, "we will put some alcohol on it," and led him towards the dorm.

Ali's face reddened to match his swollen earlobe, this was the first time in his life that a girl had voluntarily held his hand. As they turned the corner towards the building he looked down at the boys and smiled at them, and he walked the rest of that long journey to the girls' floor with his head down and his left hand cupping his ear, throwing sidelong glances at Rana.

When they reached the staircase landing leading to the girls' floor, Ali began to drag his feet and pull his hand free from Rana's. She gripped his hand with both her hands and continued to pull him towards the door. "Help me get him in," she told Naseem and they each took one arm and started to pull him through the doorway. By now Ali's ears had turned beet red, and he had a serious look on his face. He looked constipated. He was going where no boy had gone before, and he was going to be changed forever if he let them drag him inside their bedroom. He tried to pull them down by relaxing his muscles and weighing himself down, but the fact that he was weightless did not help him much. He was dragged in effortlessly by the giggling girls. Rana closed the door behind him and stood by Naseem to see what he would do next. Ali looked around the room wide-eyed. It was arranged exactly like the boys' room below it—the same row of beds, same lockers, and the same three tall windows, but Ali was inspecting it as if it was the interior of a spaceship. Naseem went to Fatima's room to look for the rubbing alcohol and left Rana with Ali.

"This is my bed," Rana pointed to the bed near the window.

"That's where my bed is too," Ali said excitedly, "I'm right under you!"

Naseem returned with some paper tissues and a bottle of alcohol. She gave them to Rana, who soaked the tissue with the alcohol and dabbed Ali's swollen earlobe with it. He jerked his head back and sucked the air in reaction to the burn. Rana applied more alcohol, but this time, she blew on his ear to soothe the burn, which made Ali shiver. Rana and Naseem looked at each other and began to giggle. Ali's face became flushed again and he wiped his ear on his shoulder. Rana set the bottle and the tissue on the floor and whispered something to Naseem. "No!" Naseem protested.

"Come on, do it for me," Rana insisted.

"Alright," Naseem reluctantly agreed, "I don't know what's your story these days."

Then they both grabbed Ali again and began pulling him inside the room. Ali didn't fight them this time, but when they reached the foot of Rana's bed, and she started to pull his hand out, he started stiffening up again.

"Don't be afraid," Rana said, "I just want you to touch my bed."

Ali's knees became weak and he surrendered himself to his fate. He reached out without help and pressed his hand on the white cover sheet. He looked up and smiled proudly at the girls.

"You're pretty pleased with yourself now," Naseem said, looking disgusted.

Ali surveyed the room with great pride and asked her, "Which one is your bed?"

Naseem looked at Rana and hissed, "Don't you dare!"

Ali broke away from them and touched every bed in the room. The girls chased after him, over and under the beds, until he stopped at the windows and started calling out to the boys in the courtyard. Mustapha and Jaguar looked up to see Ali, hands clenched together in a show of victory. As the girls wrestled him away from the window the boys watched in amusement, counting the floors, again and again, to confirm that he was indeed where they thought he was. Ali might as well have been standing on the top of Mt. Everest.

In the late afternoon, the kids started getting hungry. The school hadn't been able to provide the usual afternoon snack of biscuits and lemonade during the siege. So every day around this time the kids would go scavenging for food. The best catch so far had been three packets of creamy Chocomo that Ali managed to steal from a general store during a lull from the fighting. The store was already broken into and abandoned, so it was a breeze for Ali to get in.

In the morning, Jaguar overheard a neighbor tell Fatima that the bakery across the street from the back gate had finally shut down. The baker had grown tired of trying to open up during the lulls. The last straw had been when shrapnel shattered the bakery window. Jaguar told Ali about the incident, and they snuck out of the back gate to see if they could get some bread. They crawled behind the barricades while the militiamen listened to the radio. The volume was turned up to full blast, and ABBA's "Knowing Me Knowing You" was rattling the windows in the nearby apartments. They came upon the door of the bakery and jiggled the doorknob, but it didn't turn. Jaguar peeked inside the store, shielding his face from the sun's reflection. Then he saw it—a voluptuous mound of fresh dough, all powdered with flour, lying right next to the broken window.

"Give me a boost!" he said excitedly.

Ali cupped his hands and Jaguar stepped on them and reached in through the soccer ball-sized hole in the window. He started scooping the dough, pulling it out through the glass, and stuffing it down his shirt, through the collar, and down to his belly. When his shirt was filled to capacity, they ducked and ran back into the school. They found Mustapha, Rana, and Naseem and showed them the loot.

"Bravo," exclaimed Naseem sarcastically, obviously disappointed. "I thought you were going to get some bread. You have to cook this stuff, you donkey," she snapped at Jaguar, who stared in confusion down at his flour-stained pregnant belly.

"That's not a problem," said Ali, and he ran up to his room and came back with five empty Kiwi shoe polish cans.

"We'll cook them in these," he said proudly, looking up at Rana to see if she was impressed with his inventiveness.

Ali led them to the adjacent courtyard for the elementary school classrooms, where the counselor couldn't see them, and they settled in the corner of one of the U-shaped balconies that connected the classrooms. He told Mustapha about a broken chair he saw in the history class upstairs and asked him to break off some pieces from it and bring them down so that they could start a fire. They lit the fire using matches that Ali had stolen from the kitchen the day before, and they stooped around it like desert nomads. Each of them packed their can with dough and placed it directly on the fire. What they ended up with was dried-up dough, but at least it was something fresh. They sat around pinching little pieces from the cans and chewing them like gum.

As they sat there quietly nibbling away, they heard the rhythmic drumming of boots along with intermittent barking of orders. It was the Phalangists coming in for an evening training session. They jogged across the upper courtyard and down the stairs to settle in the lower one. As they went past, Jaguar peeked out from the hiding place to take a look at them. Mustapha immediately pulled him in by his shirt collar and told him to stay put. All of the kids could see the change in Mustapha's face as he moved back further into the corner; they'd never seen him look vulnerable before. They went back to eating; quietly listening to the echoes of the pep rally. Every few minutes one of the kids would pop their head up to check if there was anybody around.

"Here, take this and put it on," Naseem said, taking off a small necklace with a cross that she always wore concealed under her clothes, and extending it to Mustapha.

Mustapha took it and held it, looking puzzled.

"Why are you giving it to him?" asked Jaguar.

"To protect him. They wouldn't take him away if they thought he was Christian."

"But he is Christian," said Jaguar, happy to be ahead of Naseem for a change. "It's just that he is Palestinian," explained Jaguar, "the Phalangists are against the Palestinians, not the Moslems."

"But I hear that the Christians and the Moslems are killing each other too," she replied.

"That's what I hear too," confirmed Ali.

"You don't know anything. The Phalangists want to kick the Palestinians out of Beirut, that's why they are fighting," insisted Jaguar.

"Well, I want him to keep the cross anyway" replied Naseem.

"I thought Mustapha was a Moslem name," Rana said.

"I don't know but I guess it can be both," said Ali, "but if they ask me for my name I'm not going to tell them that it's Ali because Fatima told me that they might cut my throat on the spot if they know that."

"Here you could take my cross. I have another one," said Jaguar, handing over his cross to Ali, "but I'm telling you, it's not going to make any difference."

"What is Rana?" asked Ali.

"I don't know," answered Rana.

"What…" he began to prod further, but before he could finish his inquiry he saw Michel and two other young men in full military garb staring down at them. Michel had his thumbs hooked in his belt with a cigarette sticking out of one hand. He was staring right at Mustapha.

"Come here, I want to ask you a question," he called to him. Mustapha crawled slowly out of the corner and stood in front of Michel, his hand raised in front of him.

"What are you afraid of darling?" Michel said then he faked a jab at him and made a kissing sound that startled Mustapha. "We're all brothers, right. There is nothing to be afraid of." He took another sip of his cigarette. "Open your mouth just a little bit," he said lazily, blowing the smoke in Mustapha's face. The boy complied, his lips trembling and Michel knocked off the ashes of his cigarette into Mustapha's mouth. The militiamen laughed as Mustapha stood there, mouth half-open wondering whether to swallow the ashes or to spit them out. "What's your name?" Michel then asked him.

"Mustapha Ghalayini," he answered, swallowing the ashes.

"And your nationality?" Michel continued.

"Palestinian" answered Mustapha in shaky defiance. Michel slapped him across his ear and his cheek, losing his own cigarette on impact. Mustapha wiped his face with the back of his hand and looked up at Michel again only to be slapped again. Michel moved on to Ali. "And you, with the nose, what is your nationality?"

"Palestinian!" Ali burst out crying, anticipating the hurt.

Michel slapped him and moved on to Jaguar. "And you?"

"Palestinian" Jaguar replied, receiving his slap with quiet resignation.

Michel then walked up to Naseem and Rana who were holding each other. He looked down at them for a second and then turned to walk away.

"Palestinian."

"Palestinian," came two unsolicited replies one after the other.

He turned toward them for a second with a puzzled look and then turned and continued to walk away, smiling and shaking his head, followed by his friends.

The kids remained seated in silence on the classroom floor for a long while. Jaguar was patting Mustapha on the back in an effort to comfort him but Mustapha was inconsolable, swinging between whimpering laments and tearful anger.

"Big macho man he thinks he is," Mustapha cried. "Dog! Let him put down that gun for a second and let him spend a minute alone with me and I will show him! Dog! He is afraid to go outside so he is fighting the kids in here. Scrawny coward!"

Naseem, the most composed of the bunch, crawled over to Mustapha and sat kneeling opposite of him. She took out a tissue and started to wipe Mustapha's ash-rimmed lips.

"Did it burn?" she asked.

"No, it was just the ashes. They're stuck on my tongue. I can't swallow them."

"Let's get you some water Mustapha," she said, lifting Mustapha by the armpits in an attempt to prod him to stand up. This stopped Mustapha's crying because he was caught off guard by Naseem's uncharacteristic tenderness.

Jaguar and Ali helped Mustapha up and followed Naseem as she led them back to the dorm. Rana made sure that the fire was out and ran to catch up with them.

The kids had just settled in the dorm. They were all in Fatima's room, sitting on the ground and pretending to watch the television. Their emotions alternated between the nausea of trauma and the sweet sense of solidarity. They kept on stealing glances at each other, especially at Mustapha. They felt grown up, that they had aged years in the past hour. Fatima was downstairs in the kitchen.

They had seen her on their way up to her room. They didn't think twice about gathering together, the girls and the boys on the same floor in the same room without a chaperone. The consequences did not matter anymore. They wanted to be together. Suddenly Fatima burst in, huffing and puffing.

"I just got a call on the kitchen phone. They're allowing people from the outside to go into Achrafieh," she said breathlessly, "There is some sort of truce. Your relatives should be coming anytime now because the barricades have been open for the past few hours."

She ran back and forth between them and the windows to look out for any signs of traffic.

"There, you see! Look at the traffic down there! Look at the cars coming uphill. Here comes your uncle, Ali. That is your uncle's Volkswagen isn't it?" Fatima said, pulling Ali up by the shoulder. "Go pack your clothes. Just stuff them in the laundry bags. I don't know how much time we have."

Ali went to the window and let out a squeal of delight. "Uncle Abdallah!" he yelled and dashed for his room. But before he got to the doorway he stopped and looked back at Rana. "Bye," he said waving to everybody. "I'll see you next year or maybe later this year." Everybody nodded and waved silently, though somehow they sensed that they would never see each other again.

All through the twilight hours, a car would pull into the courtyard and a kid or two would run out with their laundry bags, load up and drive off. By nightfall, only Mustapha and Rana were still sitting in Fatima's room, waving goodbye from the window to people as they departed. Suha was somewhere on the Girls' floor and the principal was running between his office in the administration building and the courtyard, alternately fielding calls from parents, and saying his goodbyes. Even Fatima had left when her brother came for her. All throughout this time, the militiamen continued their training into the night in the lower courtyard. So Rana and Mustapha watched this split-screen scene below them: the joyful, tearful reunions of their friends in the upper courtyard and, in the lower one, the robotic exercises of the black-clad armed men whose barks seem to get louder and more shrill with every departure.

Rana's aunt finally arrived in an old gray Mercedes, and the principal came out to greet her as he had done with all the parents. Rana did not rush out or squeal with delight as the other kids had done. She looked at the car for a few minutes until she saw her sister Suha run out to embrace her Aunt. Then she walked out of the room and came back with her laundry bags, and stood by a puzzled Mustapha. She sidled up to him until they were standing shoulder to shoulder. They watched the lower courtyard until they heard someone shouting below them. It was Suha and she was waving her arms frantically trying to get Rana's attention. Rana mechanically acknowledged her sister and aunt with a wave and she turned to Mustapha.

"Bye. I will see you…all alright?" she said, not knowing what else to say.

"Bye," he answered, "send my regards to your mother."

"Ok," she said, her voice weakening. She put her hand on his shoulder, looked down at the lower courtyard for the last time, turned around, and left the room dragging her bags.

As they packed the trunk, Rana noticed that Mustapha had followed her out and was now standing at the main entrance of the dorm. The principal saw him and walked over to him. He put his hand on Mustapha's shoulder and began to talk to him. Mustapha did not look at him, and when the Principal patted him on the shoulder, he shook off the comforting hand and stood there, in his goalie-stance, looking at the ground. When the car pulled away, Rana saw that Mustapha was still standing alone, except that he was now facing the courtyard stairs. While her aunt was waiting to pull out of the gate, Rana looked back to see if Mustapha was still there. She saw him walk to the staircase leading down to the playground where the militiamen were training. He walked slowly down the steps, stopping to survey the scene below him, and then descended further. Now, she could see only his upper body. Now, only his head. Now, he was out of sight, and with his disappearance, she heard the orderly shouts of the militiamen breakdown into a wild ruckus.

About the Author

Zein El-Amine is a Lebanese-born poet and writer. He has an MFA in Poetry from the University of Maryland. His poems have appeared in *Wild River Review*, *Folio*, *Beltway Quarterly*, *Foreign Policy In Focus*, *CityLit*, *Graylit*, *Split This Rock*, *Penumbra*, *DC Poets Against The War: An Anthology*, and *Ghostfishing: An Eco-Justice Poetry Anthology*. His latest poetry manuscript "A Travel Guide for the Exiled" was recently shortlisted for the Bergman Prize, judged by Louise Glück. His short stories have appeared in *Uno Mas*, *Jadaliyya*, *Middle East Report*, *Wild River Review*, *About Place Journal*, and *Bound Off*.

About the Publisher

Radix Media is a worker-owned printer and publisher based in Brooklyn, New York, producing beautifully designed books and ephemera. They publish new ideas and fresh perspectives, prioritizing the voices of typically marginalized communities to get to the root of the human experience.

Their books have won awards from *Foreword Reviews* and AIGA.

Find all of their books at **radixmedia.org/our-books**.

Colophon

This book was printed with union labor by Radix Media in Brooklyn, New York, using an AB Dick 9995 offset press. The interior stock is Mohawk Via Vellum 70# text. The cover was printed on 111# Gmund cover stock.

Other Titles By Radix Media

Mortals
John Dermot Woods & Matt L.

Fanning the Flames: A Molly Crabapple Coloring Book
Molly Crabapple

The Solar Grid
Ganzeer

There Is Still Singing in the Afterlife
JinJin Xiu

BINT
Ghinwa Jawhari

We Are All Things
Elliott Colla & Ganzeer

Futures: A Science Fiction Series
Various

Be the Change! A Justseeds Coloring Book
Justseeds Artists' Cooperative, ed. Molly Fair

Aftermath: Explorations of Loss & Grief
Anthology, ed. Radix Media

Forthcoming

Many Worlds
ed. Cadwell Turnbull & Josh Eure